Rasia

Koral Dasgupta's stories appear randomly through her books, academic lectures, speeches, columns and paintings. A literary movement founded by her, www.tellmeyourstory.in, hosts short stories and poems written by people across age, professions and geographies.

As a professor of Marketing, Communications and Creative Writing, she conducts workshops and talks at educational and corporate floors. She also consults with the corporate in marketing communications and content space. She is an advisory member with CBFC Mumbai.

Rasia: The Dance of Desire is her third book.

Readers can reach her via Twitter or
Instagram @Rasia_thebook

Please feel free to tag her in your reviews, comments, thoughts on the book or photographs with the book.

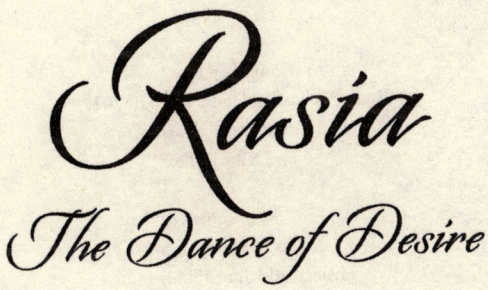
Rasia
The Dance of Desire

KORAL DASGUPTA

RUPA

Published by
Rupa Publications India Pvt. Ltd 2017
7/16, Ansari Road, Daryaganj
New Delhi 110002

Sales centres:
Allahabad Bengaluru Chennai
Hyderabad Jaipur Kathmandu
Kolkata Mumbai

Copyright © Koral Dasgupta, 2017

This is a work of fiction. Names, characters, places and incidents are either the product of the author's imagination or are used fictitiously and any resemblance to any actual person, living or dead, events or locales is entirely coincidental.

All rights reserved.
No part of this publication may be reproduced, transmitted, or stored in a retrieval system, in any form or by any means, electronic, mechanical, photocopying, recording or otherwise, without the prior permission of the publisher.

ISBN: 978-81-291-4948-0

First impression 2017

10 9 8 7 6 5 4 3 2 1

The moral right of the author has been asserted.

Printed at Thomson Press India Ltd., Faridabad

This book is sold subject to the condition that it shall not, by way of trade or otherwise, be lent, resold, hired out, or otherwise circulated, without the publisher's prior consent, in any form of binding or cover other than that in which it is published.

To my son,
Neev Tanish

Contents

Prelude: One year later ix

Once Upon a Time	1
Meanwhile, in a Different World	10
The Voice	20
The Bygone Chaos	24
On the Arabian Shore	27
The Voice	36
The Evening, Far Away	40
The Call of Destiny	46
The Voice	55
The Face of Resistance	58
The Intruder	63
The Secret Audience	66
The Black Goddess	69
Mentor at Work	76
Back to the Origin	85
A Fresh Dawn	93
The Unexpected Beginning	97
The Biography	104
The Restructuring	107
The Inevitable Path	115
A Vast Terrace	120

The Uncanny Contrast	124
The Desperate Lover	128
The Rise of Krishna	131
The Comet Rises	136
The Voice	143
Arrival of Kali	147
The Scary Disconnect	154
A Call to the Cosmos	160
The Dance of Desire	165
A New Beginning	173
The Negotiation	179
The Leopard's Focus	183
The Reckless Demand	190
The Confrontation	193
The Reunion	202
Call of the Stage	209
Dance of Desire	215
Rasia	220
The Introspection	227
Shiva's Confession	231
The Final Return	235
Acknowledgement	237

Prelude

One year later

BRIAN HERRETT
Manhattan, 2016

'Excuse me, may I?' I utter repeatedly, holding up my camera in one hand and my press card in the other. The unhappy faces that move aside are the standard response we journalists usually receive. But a press card has its advantages. Art patrons and enthusiastic audience flooding the auditorium and green rooms, frown. Ali, Sid and Arjun receive me warmly, leaving those around to wonder why I am so important. I hug them back like a proud brother, wink suggestively at the faces that stare, and march ahead.

Kala Mandir's inaugural performance in the heart of Manhattan was meant to declare that the dance academy is active and functional now. New admissions have started rolling in. The troupe is scattered all over the campus, answering questions and picking up well-deserved accolades.

Congratulatory messages had flooded in similarly months ago, when they learnt that Shekhar's Mumbai-based dance academy, Kala Mandir, was setting up a branch in Manhattan. For days, the Indian media covered little else but stories on Shekhar's inspiring life—his rags to riches story, his grit as a practising Bharatanatyam artiste, forming a troupe that stands by him like a rock, and his far-sightedness as an entrepreneur who never rested on past laurels. Shekhar did not have time to contribute to those stories, or to even read them. The correspondents gathered their content from sources best known to them.

But where is Shekhar?

At one corner Manasi is busy talking to some delegates from the United Nations. I reach out to her. She smiles.

'Where have you hidden Shekhar?' I whisper in her ears.

'Leave him alone, Herrett.' Manasi whispers back ignoring my joke.

Did the lady just advise a journalist to stay away from news? If Shekhar needs to be away from this chaos at such an important moment, then there is a story brewing somewhere!

The OOH TV planted above runs some channels from India and the USA, lavishly praising the event and the one who made it all possible.

'Ideals. Ambition. Pace. Discipline. And a ruthless drive to dismiss whatever is not to be. These are a few words that describe Raj Shekhar Subramanian,' declares the excited young lady on the screen. She calls him a huge inspiration in the Indian cultural space.

I double back, my eyes scanning the crowd for the 'inspiration', ignoring the wife's injunction to leave him alone. I invite disapproving glances as I push through the crowd again, my body further encumbered by a huge bag and a camera on the side.

The show has ended about an hour ago. This is when Shekhar openly interacts with all the delegates and audience, carefully observing every minute detail of their reactions and responses. His absence at this hour can't be a silly exception.

I touch the bag loosely hanging from my shoulders and hold it closer to myself. Then I briskly walk out of the hall.

There he stands, at an isolated corner of the corridor in the rear end of the auditorium. He has just washed his face to remove all makeup. The trident painted elaborately on his back is now covered with a shawl. Having been a friend to Shekhar for eight years now, I know when not to make my presence felt. More so because he has been trying to avoid me of late. But this situation has left me confused. Maybe I should risk it.

'What's the fun soaking in the accolades alone, Shekhar? Let's do it together over wine,' I say, interrupting his reverie. Shekhar turns around and smiles pleasantly.

I look behind, wondering whether the stern lips have curved for me or it's directed at someone else. Sceptically, I look back at him. After being neglected for a while with condescending cynicism, the unpredictable warmth feels rattling. This strange man had maintained a distance ever since I pronounced my plans. He had interpreted my proposal as an obscene uninvited encroachment into his private space.

'Am I hallucinating or are you really in a mood to say yes?' I ask in disbelief.

'I am prepared, Brian.' He says. 'You can go ahead.'

Still stunned over his capitulation, I pull out some papers from my bag in haste and hand them to him.

'I am carrying the contract. I have already told you what it holds. Read well before…!'

Shekhar has signed on the dotted line even before I can finish my sentence. He holds out the papers at me. It takes a few minutes to overcome the deafening silence and find my voice.

'Has the earth been hit by a comet? India defeated Pakistan in cricket? Has the US president called you to spend a night at the White House?' I ramble along. 'What's wrong with you, Shekhar? I had been chasing you for days to write your biography, and you had steadfastly denied to have anything to do with it until yesterday. What changed this evening?'

Shekhar looks away. 'I need to unburden some secrets of my life, Brian. Maybe I will, when I reveal myself,' he says.

I know where this pensiveness comes from.

Here he stands, all alone, hiding himself from the adulation due to him at the end of what seems to be the most life-altering show of his career. But neither the media, nor his friends and well-wishers, nor Shekhar himself could have predicted an evening which will make him stand at a crossroads, questioning everything that he has ever believed! Two women wait for him at two different ends of the crossroads. He knows which path is his, but he can't walk that path till he has attended to the other. I wait, watching him introspect silently over a long journey; eventful and interesting, successful yet self-defeating.

Finally, he turns to face me. Those ever-energetic eyes look tired.

'We can start tomorrow, if you are ready,' he affirms.

In the next moment he is gone, leaving me bewildered. I repeatedly check whether Shekhar has really signed the contract without reading it. That is so not like him.

This biography would be interesting, I tell myself; more so, if Shekhar remains this vulnerable and is vocal about the unexpected and unexplored facets of his being. He must have been touched beyond measure by the success of the inaugural event. He had been aiming to expand Kala Mandir beyond borders for a long time now. Even a rock melts after such an achievement.

And, there is something more than what meets the eye here.

I press the signed contract papers against my mouth and announce dramatically, 'Raj Shekhar Subramanian, we may now kiss the bride!'

1

Once Upon a Time

VATSALA PANDIT
Manhattan, 2015

I kick open the door of my damned attic room. It's about time that the office pays for a bigger apartment. I am way too bored with the same wall, floor, ceiling and the view outside my window. And I'm too tired to pick up the bag, glares, shoes and belts hurled all across the floor. I throw myself on the bed, push the laptop away. Why can't I have trained personnel for these meaningless chores? I am not meant for these.

In fact, I am meant for something else; someone else. I am meant for a body that can create celestial images with the torso; hands that titillate the air; ornaments that glitter like the sun; feet that threaten to wake the indifferent earth; music that beats like the pounding of the heart. The speed, the power, the captivating energy, rebirth of the body with each new posture…

Few years ago, a new dance troupe from India called Kala Mandir had come to New York for a performance. The hoardings showed a man from the back, his hands bent with a bow and arrow pointing upwards. Two feminine hands appeared crisscrossing on his bare back, displaying some erect dance posture. One hand was stained in red and adorned with intricate jewellery; the other was plain and barren.

Typical Indian chauvinism in the advertisements. But a fatal curiosity drew me towards the auditorium.

The show was obscurely titled 'Manipur Stotram'. I was told that the troupe had been a huge name in Southeast Asia lately; it was fast emerging as a significant cultural icon.

'Cultural icon, eh?' I had thought contemptuously. 'A little popularity prompts people to pour out the most lavish appreciation. They don't take much time to dump their "icons" either. When you don't have it in you to make a difference, you clumsily look around for heroes!'

This was the story of Arjun and Chitrangada. Before the show started, pamphlets were handed over to us so we knew what was coming up. I threw mine away. Someone from the crowd prompted that the tale was from an Indian epic.

So this was the brave third Pandava who might appreciate a woman's brilliance at archery and defence skills but looks for physical beauty in a woman he would wed. Chitrangada, the warrior princess from Manipur, fell in love with Arjun and became pretty after seeking assistance from the Gandharv* Maya. Maya transformed her into a sensuous woman who could arouse a man's desire with her beauty. Arjun fell in love with her and proposed marriage. Chitrangada re-introduced herself as the Kshatriya woman whom he had once rejected. She put forth the condition that Arjun could marry her only if he'd respect

---

*Gandharv: heavenly beings referred to in ancient texts of Hinduism and Buddhism

her for being what she was. Arjun relented.

A lot changed in those ninety minutes.

Within the close confines of my home I tried to recreate some of the postures in front of the mirror. When my attempts reflected not even a fraction of what I had witnessed, I kicked whatever lay in front of me in sheer frustration. The next day, I went back to watch the same show once again, with my veins thrilling to this unique charm. I felt feverish. The costumes, that divine body language, the melody and music, light and beauty, and God himself, placed magnificently in between.

The show haunted me for days after it was over.

In 'Manipur Stotram', Maya, the Gandharv, creates an optical illusion to transform Chitrangada into a beautiful, sensuous woman. When Chitrangada invited the Gandharv to transform her, the girl representing her beautiful form entered the stage and took position right in front of the leading lady. The two women performed a twin-dance as if they were one. As if the lady dancing behind was a shadow of the girl in front.

What creative brilliance!

The potrayal of Arjun's dilemma was intense. With chaste movements Raj Shekhar Subramanian displayed the internal conflict of aligning between beauty and brains, equivalent to choosing between weakness and strength. Beauty is the ultimate genesis of a man's longing, whereas a talented woman would assist him to move forward and conquer. Subramanian used his slender body to emote Arjun's dilemma with enthusiastic restlessness, elegance and fast movements, presenting a passionate rendition before his audience.

For years I have been a practising ballet dancer. Ballet is peaceful and serene. Balance and restrain are the key. What I saw on stage that day, however, was vigorous and energetic, defying all restraint. Here, you don't just merely seek; you demand. You force the passive to sit up and take notice. The aggression with which the feet fell on the ground, producing their own musical rhythm, seemed to threaten the forces of the cosmos.

I wanted to acquire that vigour, the energy, the power to threaten the inevitable, the beauty that transforms and intimidates, and yet leaves you longing for more! After the performance, when the press and adoring fans mobbed the Dancer, I waited, lost in the crowd, watching him, awestruck and motionless.

That was my space. That was what I had been looking for. I felt within me an overwhelming need to embrace this art form. And I must learn it from none other than Raj Shekhar Subramanian.

I heard the Dancer say, '"Manipur Stotram" was our first show in India. It gave us fame and accolades. Manasi planted the theme one evening, while narrating and translating Rabindranath Tagore's *Chitrangada*.' I enquired and understood that Manasi was his wife, the woman who played Chitrangada. I turned back to Subramanian. Tall, fair and elegant. Smiled less but seemed pleasant. His body was lean, tough and well-toned.

'The show was initially launched at Rabindrasadan, Kolkata,' a stupid guy from his PR team blurted out to the over-enthusiastic crowd surrounding him. 'The city, sensitive to anything that refers to Tagore, did not criticize Kala Mandir for naming the poet's famous dance drama as its inspiration. Instead, art enthusiasts had a resurrection of sorts as their eyes were glued to the stage and they offered a standing ovation at the end of the performance. The next day, all the dailies were flooded with appreciation for the performance. Shekhar's phone never stopped ringing. Most of the reputed theatres across the country that had given him a tough time disagreeing, semi-agreeing and finally reluctantly agreeing to give him slots for limited days, eventually extended the contract due to the stupendous public response.'

The PR guy smiled as if he was talking about himself. What he said next though, was what I wanted to hear. 'Shekhar wants to set up branches of Kala Mandir in other cities across the world, including Manhattan.'

Since then, I had been following their YouTube videos regularly and kept myself informed with everything that Kala Mandir was up to.

Last year, the troupe came to New York once again to perform at the New York International Fringe Festival. For all the seven days that they had performed, they received immense appreciation. Not a single ticket was wasted. This time I got myself a VIP pass to be closer to the Dancer. The crowd rushed towards the performers after the show was over. I watched him speak with non-committal politeness. Patiently he charmed the media, accepting praise with grace and rehashing responses when questions were repeated. He was expressive and articulate, but discreet. His eyes had the lustre of the triumphant; confidence and dominance took their rounds even when he was silent. And he was observant. All through the evening I stared at the Dancer. Once in between the conversations, he looked back at me. His eyes communicated neither approval nor disapproval;

he just coldly and emotionlessly registered that I was ogling at him, acknowledging the information with indifference.

I needed to feature in his scheme of things; I needed to do it fast. Hours spent in dumb awe were hours wasted. I tried to seek an appointment. Each time I was told that Subramanian was too busy to indulge in 'purposeless conversations'.

A common problem with the big dads of any industry is that they assume before they take pains to understand. But I made peace with it, aware that I could not be the only one asking for a meeting with the famous Raj Shekhar Subramanian. Finally, the day after their last show in New York, when the team had dispersed to go around the city, and the Dancer was standing alone on the balcony of his hotel, I managed to pass on a sealed envelope through the room service staff, with instructions that it be delivered only to Raj Shekhar Subramanian. I was told that he had opened my note with the greatest reluctance.

Hi Mr Subramanian,

I have been following your YouTube videos to train myself in Bharatanatyam. I learnt the steps from your performances, tried to copy your expressions, and also memorized the music. If you play them for me now, I can sleepwalk through them.

I am drawn to this art because of the rhythm that resonates when you perform, your control over muscles and the way you balance your body on earth, while your mind encapsulates various roles, all so simultaneously. The feet keeping to time, hands expressing gestures, eyes following the hands with expressions, ears responding to the music and the sixth sense of the performer guiding his impulses all through, are skills I have mastered watching your performances.

If one of your dancers falls ill before a show, you could call me. I would enact the bit flawlessly.

I have copied you as much as I could from your recorded shows. I now wish to unlearn all of that and reorganize my basics. I want to learn it from you. Walk me into your world, Mr Subramanian. I have been waiting for months.

Love,
Vatsala Pandit

What came back to me in response was only one line, scrawled by hand, saying, 'If Kala Mandir ever comes to the US, you will be the first student I'll consider.'

One little careless sentence in return of a piece of my heart? No invitation to test the talent I claimed to possess? My body cringed; my ears grew hot. I wanted to smash something to release that hopeless energy.

He had discounted the stars in my eyes as filth, coming from some moronic, attention-seeking novice! How dare he think that I would go back home kissing his handwriting, happy with the autograph and his empty assurance? Indians perceive politeness as the resort of the weak. Aggression works better on them, especially the ones that brutally show them their place. This time, a stern note reached the Dancer, challenging his nonchalance.

I know, Sir, that fans and followers are never respected. They are considered to be nameless, faceless, inconsistent and wannabes! These creatures are supposed to be seen off from a distance; maybe granted a smile, a hug, a wave or a photograph together—and you are done.

You have treated my deepest urge like a joke; I'll treat your joke like the biggest truth of my life. Not far is the day when we will stand facing each other right here on the plains of Manhattan. I will remind you of your promise then.

Avoid, if you can!

Yours,
Vatsala

I didn't know what to do next. In burning rage, I had thrown together whatever words occurred to me, to insult him like he had insulted me. I am certainly not the one who could be discarded like an old newspaper. I was not born to die without giving a befitting response to humiliation.

I came to know that the snob had crumpled my second note and thrown it in the dustbin. He had instructed the staff not to deliver anything from the same source again.

I had smiled, though it set my blood boiling in rage. Yes, I *had* reached out unsolicited, but that didn't make me a beggar! I deserved what I demanded! And I would prove that to him.

It was a frustrating, but interesting turn of events. Chasing what the heart desires is a lot more exciting than when it simply comes to you unbidden, as a gift. I left the hotel with a resolve to not let this person die till he had taught me Bharatanatyam.

For days after, I actively searched for a way forward with a vengeance. It was both my dream and destiny that I chose to walk this path, with zero assurance from any corner. I carved my own relentless way forward, galloping towards the reckless Indian artiste.

Today he stands not too far away.

Very soon his phone will receive a call from the Department of Cultural Affairs, New York, and they'll make him an offer he can't refuse!

Jesus, I feel like the Godfather. Wicked, ambitious and unforgiving.

2

Meanwhile, in a Different World

RAJ SHEKHAR SUBRAMANIAN
Thiruvananthapuram, 2015

The paint has faded, the grills are rusty, green and black moss grows thick on the walls of this old building, standing on the outskirts of Thiruvananthapuram. Some cement has been applied in patches to the walls to mend whatever cracks have appeared, after standing strong for years without any maintenance. There is a garden in the front of the building. It is overgrown with weeds and cries out for maintenance. A steep, dark stairway leads upstairs, to the rooms where the children sleep. The first floor also has a shabby balcony, half of which is occupied by a broken table feasted upon by insects, with chairs without legs hurled on top. Everything about the place suggests that this is a very old orphanage struggling for existence.

I sit on the roughly hewn stairs with the warden, Jacob Kollipara, watching kids play in the small lawn in the front of the building.

'What brings you here again, Shekhar?' asks JK.

'You know what brings me here.'

JK stares at me in silence for a brief while. 'Why haven't you grown out of that shabby bed in the small room that you once occupied? The beds in your house now must give you much better dreams.'

'Some nightmares are closer to you than your best dreams, JK.'

JK speaks again after a short pause. 'Your wife came here, when you had come to Kerala last time for that conference. Very nice girl.'

This takes me off-guard. 'Manasi came here? When? And why? You never told me. Neither did she. What did she say?'

'She asked me not to tell you. She came here to visit the orphanage which sheltered her husband during his younger days. She wanted to see the room you shared with other kids, the bed that you slept on…' Jacob Sir goes on, but I have stopped listening. Manasi's childhood and mine are as disparate as chalk and cheese. What would she understand of this place?

I brush aside the thought and look around. The orphanage can't decay and turn into a heap of ruins. It has to stay. The memories in this house are all that I have of my childhood. Those are my parents, my siblings and my anchor in every sense.

'How much more do you need to finish the repairs, Jacob Sir?' I ask.

JK shakes his head. 'How much more would you give, Shekhar? Every month I already receive generous amounts from you for the nutrition and well-being of the kids. Shekhar, this is an orphanage. As much as you give, there will still be something missing, the void of which no one can ever fill.'

Sad and lost, I hang my head downwards. JK doesn't let the silence reign.

'How is Ali?' he asks.

I assure him that Ali is doing great, and mentally prepare myself to respond to the advice that is coming up.

JK bends closer. 'Shekhar, you should come here more often. Talk to them; inspire them. Induct more kids from the orphanage into your troupe, just like you did with Ali. Why do you need students from outside when you have this house to fill your team with?'

A ball hits the wall between us. JK shouts curses at the culprit. I pick it up and toss it across to the boy. He catches it with an innocent smile. He doesn't take offense to JK's rudeness, just like I didn't when I was his age.

JK is looking at me expectantly. Not that he doesn't know my stand. But he continues to say the same thing every time I am here. He thinks my affluence can take care of all these homeless ill-destined children and the burden on the orphanage can reduce. But I can't do this. However crude it may sound, Kala Mandir is my dance academy, not another orphanage. I open my mouth to disappoint him again.

'No Jacob sir; my feelings for this home and passion for Bharatanatyam are pretty exclusive. I cannot merge the two. Only those who dance for the joy of it can come with me. I cannot trade for bread some forced interest out of these kids.'

The stench of the open drain outside enters my nostrils as I take a deep breath. I may have travelled very far, yet I will never feel alien in these surroundings. It disturbs me, but nothing can prevent me from coming back.

I continue, 'They are all very well aware of my name and work. Let them approach me by themselves if they wish to. But yes, they will have to fulfill all the entrance formalities to reach me. Ali did that. He didn't expect favours. The fact that they share the room and bed which were once mine, doesn't qualify them for anything.'

I look back at JK. 'If you treat them like poor underprivileged people today then that's what they will always be. Poor and underprivileged.'

My voice is firm and conclusive. JK lets out a deep sigh. I still try my best to offer help. 'Should I appoint someone who can assist you with things here? I will pay his salary.'

JK scowls. 'I don't want one more dependent to be a leech on me. They call me old and haggard already. A new guy would mean they'll not listen to me at all. I'll be left alone to die.'

I smile at his apprehension. At a very basic level, we all have the same fears. That space where we are unchallenged, empowered and forever supported, the pedestal we have built for ourselves over the years, however big or small, must never slip away from our grip.

I get up to bid JK goodbye and start for the airport. He grimly utters, 'God bless you.'

∽

On my flight back to Mumbai, I look outside the window.

Why did Manasi visit the orphanage? Why this unnecessary interest in my past? Why the secrecy?

These are some weird little things that Manasi often does,

to pull me out of comfort.

Manasi!

My entire being arouses with a protective shield towards this woman. Seventeen years of togetherness is a long time. When have I ever been a husband who wakes up, orders breakfast, takes bath, goes to office, watches television, has dinner and kisses the wife goodnight? Manasi isn't tired of my creative whims. At least, not yet. Rather, the unpredictability keeps her entertained. My demure wife though, has her own ways to follow her mind. Without the least warning, she goes ahead with things without considering the consequences they might have on me and everyone else around her. Just like her secret visit to my orphanage. Just like she had agreed to marry me on an impulse, even though I had promised her neither luxury nor riches nor undying romance, as suitors usually do.

What a strange evening it was when I saw her for the first time.

That was 1998. I had landed up in Kolkata for my final round of meetings with Britannia Industries. I was being absorbed by the organization in their supply chain wing post my B.Tech. The city was celebrating the Saptami day of Durga Puja, and was all decked up in pomp and gaiety. Every lane was crowded. After finishing the formalities with Britannia, I was walking leisurely through Rashbihari Avenue watching people pouring into the sari shops, pampering themselves.

So lucky—this privileged class!

I had broken free from my orphanage and moved to the college hostel when I was sixteen. I topped various examinations at all academic levels. The Government, since then, had taken special care of me. I thrived on scholarships for a large part of my life. That made life easier, but I never had the opportunity to splurge. My funds were limited, and I had vast plans with the money I had for the days to come.

The sun had set; darkness was slowly taking over. The city, with its lamps and lights, seemed to awaken to welcome the evening festivities. Distracted with my thoughts, I had unmindfully landed up at one of the pandals,* lit brightly, surging with visitors. I made my way through the chaos and pushed myself forward. A young girl in her early twenties, flawlessly draped in a cotton saree, was dancing with the dhaak** that played. Her vigour wasn't impaired by the growing crowd watching her. I could tell from her moves that she wasn't professionally trained. Yet, she had a style—of youth and feminine abundance, of letting go and not holding back. She smiled as she stretched, bent and whirled around; her muscles and body reflected serene fulfilment. Her eyes, beneath a big maroon bindi, sparkled with mischief.

The girl had stained her feet in red. Alta, the local people called it. Her hands and neck were adorned with simple gold jewellery. She was not too fair; huge eyes and thin lips outshone every other feature of her body.

'Who is she?' asked a fat, middle-aged woman standing behind me.

A thin, younger lady responded, 'Manasi; daughter of Nobarun Bhattacharya, the priest of the puja.'

---

*Pandal: a temporary temple made to house deities during festivals
**Dhaak: special kind of drum used in Bengal, especially during Puja festivities

The first lady smirked. 'Oh! Thakur Moshai's* daughter? Why isn't she as fair as her father, then? Had she been fairer she would have been pretty. She is as thin as a grasshopper.' She covered her mouth with the corner of her sari and giggled.

The other lady made a face. 'She can dance because she is thin. Had it been you, the stage would break and Ma Durga would leave for the heavens three days before the scheduled departure.'

The smile faded from the fat woman's face. 'I would never be dancing like that in public! Hasn't Thakur Moshai taught her some decorum? No culture, no manners, poor upbringing!' She looked back at the stage angrily and then spat, 'Disgusting!'

She turned to leave and almost fell upon me. She glared as if I was responsible for the unsought collision and disappeared.

Not that I understood any bit of their language back then, but from whatever I heard I could make out a few things about the girl. My brain was racing. I kept my attention settled with her, as she abruptly stopped, gasping heavily.

The breathlessness, the perspiration that soaked her forehead and neck, her chest rising and falling, mouth open to draw in extra air—I knew those after-effects of an adrenaline rush, just after someone has danced her heart out. Who knows whether she lifted the end of her sari to wipe the sweat off her neck or to bury her face behind it! But pleasure shone through her pretence of guilt.

Following her eyes, I found an old man glaring back at her. The abrupt halt was in response to his angry gaze. Slowly, he

---

*Thakur Moshai: Bengali term for priest

shifted his eyes and walked ahead to offer the evening puja. The girl stood in a corner watching his devotions, oblivious that she was being intently followed by a stranger. The old man finished in an hour's time. Both father and daughter reached out for the dhanuchi.* I pushed myself further to watch this right from the front, annoying the people around. Together they performed the famed dhanuchi dance of Durga Puja, coordinating beautifully with each other. At one point they balanced a dhanuchi on each hand and one on their mouth. The crowd cheered. As they jumped, swung and whirled round, not even a tiny bit of burning fibre came out of the lamp.

I knew this was the girl I wanted to marry.

After the evening rituals were over, father and daughter walked back home. I walked a few steps behind them. He still looked upset. Manasi kept her head held down. The elderly person had been scolding her all through the way.

'How many times have I warned that you should not be dancing with the dhaak in an open pandal? There are so many nasty eyes around. Don't do this in my absence at least. But no, you won't listen. Something happens to you when you hear that evening dhaak. Shameless girl!'

They reached home through the narrow bylanes of Kolkata, washed their hands in the tap fitted at the entrance and entered the courtyard. I waited outside for half an hour, sipping a sugar syrup which the roadside stall called 'tea'.

A little later, I knocked on their door, hoping that they would have rested sufficiently by then. I introduced myself as a

---

*Dhanuchi: big earthen lamps burning coconut fibre and camphor to emit fragrance and smoke

professional, new to the city, who was scheduled to leave by the 11.30 p.m. train from Howrah. They welcomed me to the living room of the old bungalow, reflecting the architecture of British Bengal. I didn't waste any time in putting forth my marriage proposal. The appointment letter from Britannia Industries, coupled with my IIT-Madras background, was sufficient to enamour them.

Nobarun Bhattacharya looked at me from top to bottom. Many hardships had chiselled my personality to the extent that I couldn't be taken casually. The women of the house exchanged glances. The old man calmly asked, 'Who are you, my son?'

Everyone was stiff as steel. I took a deep breath, 'I am not someone who ever lived with a beautiful family like you have here.' I smiled at everyone. 'I am an orphan; I don't know who my parents were. I grew up in an orphanage and later in college hostels. Since then I have been on my own. But as you can see,' I pointed at my appointment letter, 'I have done well for myself.'

I stopped to drink the glass of water that had been served. As the liquid made its way down my throat, I found the old man fumbling for a response. I put the glass down, took the priest's hands into mine and looked at him in the eye.

'You don't have to say a yes or no right now, Thakur Moshai. Please think it over. I understand it is not easy to give your daughter to someone like me, with no roots or family or inherited wealth.' I paused. 'Verify my background and anything else that you wish to. You may decide thereafter.'

I sat back into my seat again. 'But before I leave, I have a request. I wish to speak to your daughter in isolation, before the family decides upon our destiny.'

A gentle murmur passed through the women. Everyone was taken aback with my shameless straightforward demand. But I wasn't looking at any of them. Nobarun Bhattacharya stared for a while, then advised his wife to arrange this meeting in one of the rooms upstairs.

I was quick to speak my mind the moment Manasi entered the room and sat down on the adjoining couch.

'The appointment letter I showed your father will not define me for more than five years. It was just an excuse to meet you,' I had said, surprising her. 'My future lies in Bharatanatyam. I have learnt the best and the purest form of art from Late Shri Kritadhi Iyer, the renowned performer of India. He came to my school for a workshop when I was in the eighth standard and has mentored me ever since. I will work for five years to save up funds and then set up my own establishment. Post that, I'll explore my journey as a dancer.'

Manasi's eyes were fixed on the floor when she had entered the room. God knows when they changed position to settle upon me with a bold assurance.

'Come aboard only if you agree to this. I'll teach you my art. Then, we can set up our team together and write our own destiny.'

I got up. She remained seated, her eyes bright; or so I felt.

3

The Voice

Shekhar didn't ask anything more of Manasi; neither did he wait for Manasi to clarify the doubts she may have had. He left, leaving his address in Bangalore, where he would be posted for the initial months of his job. He also wrote down for me all the details of his upbringing, each institute with its address, so that we could satisfy ourselves by verifying these details. As he walked out of the main gate, Manasi came out to stand on the first floor balcony, watching him from above. Shekhar glanced back at her.

I understood she had accepted his proposal.

As soon as he left, the women of the clan sprang upon Manasi demanding to know what had happened inside the room, to which she smiled mischievously. 'He asked if I can cook, wash clothes and dry them, and clean and maintain a house. And most importantly, he asked whether I have learnt to spend money or to preserve it.'

With squeals of laughter following these words she fled from there, but not before sharing a brief look with me. I instantly knew that she was bluffing!

Late in the night the sound of crickets seemed too loud to put to rest my tense nerves. Lost deep into my thoughts, I relaxed on the rocking chair inside my room. My wife Sharda was cleaning our bed. She noticed the silence.

'What are you thinking?' she asked.

'About the boy, obviously!' I turned to face the window and kept talking, half to her and half to myself.

'See, I am no old fashioned fossil. I have been working with SAIL for many years and have travelled to many places, gaining new experiences and shedding prejudices. We have brought up our only daughter with a lot of care; now we want a deserving boy who would respect her talents and understand her innocence. This sudden proposal from a stranger has surprised me, but I appreciate that the boy did not walk up to my daughter like many others in the pandal. Reaching out to the family means seriousness in his intentions. I have my doubts, though, that just a few moments of watching a girl can arouse marital instincts in a modern, educated, well-to-do guy. However, such things are not unheard of either.'

The wife stopped me from ranting any further. 'Don't forget that he has an excellent academic background, and a fantastic job in hand. That means a bright future. Manasi will live the life of a queen. Such proposals won't come by every day!'

I agreed, 'True. But what worries me is that the boy has no family. Who would be there for Manasi immediately after marriage? She'd be rudely thrown into the bare practicalities of life too soon. Building up a family all alone is not easy. It would pain me to see my daughter giving up her romantic dreams way too early!'

I looked at the lace cloth spread on the table in the corner of the room. 'Remember, you weaved this when we were newly married? You could enjoy your time with me. These were some little things you did to create the home of your choice. Today Manasi knows what books I read; I don't have to tell her but she keeps them on my table.'

I bent to touch the flowers in the vase. 'She loves to bring these home and adorn her favourite corners. I want her to be able to do these things. She shouldn't have to get sucked into cooking and providing right from the first day!'

I may have sounded a bit too agitated. Sharda smiled. 'Patience. Do you think the boy will subject her to household chores and drudgery all at once? Is that why he wants to marry her? He wants a wife to feed him and take care of the house, now that he has a job?'

'Not really.' I let out a deep sigh. 'There's something else to it. He has said something to Manasi which has won her heart.' I pondered for a while. 'I don't really have a reason to complain. He answered honestly and transparently to everything I asked him. My experienced eyes recognized Shekhar as honest and true to his faith. Our personalities match in more ways than one.'

I smiled at Sharda. 'Maybe I'm being overprotective about my daughter. I had better stop my old, wandering mind and verify the boy's background discreetly. We'll talk about this if everything seems right.'

It was about time that I hit the bed. I chose to take a walk on the balcony before calling it a day. Two doors away, I stood at the entrance to my daughter's room.

While we were actively discussing the whirlwind turn of events, Manasi had been stealthily smiling, alone in her room. She had settled herself on a window seat, braiding and unbraiding her hair unmindfully, looking outside at the half-arched moon, building up dreams and aspirations for a different world.

I stood there motionless, watching her.

Soon, we were done with our verification of Shekhar's background. In an elaborate traditional Bengali wedding, the two were declared man and wife.

Seventeen years have passed since then. In these seventeen years, my daughter and son-in-law have created history, and a large part of history that had once been very dear to them has faded out from the face of earth, maintaining its relevance only in memories.

4

The Bygone Chaos

BRIAN HERRETT
Manhattan, 2016

'Shekhar,' I interrupt. 'This sounds like a classic Indian love story. I never thought you could fall in love at first sight!'

Sitting with Shekhar recording and taking down notes as he narrates his past comes with its own perils. A breezy weekend morning like this one merits a can of beer. But Shekhar is in a trance. Who demands beer from the goose that is laying golden eggs?

The guest house is calm and serene, missing that familiar chaos it experienced for the last few months. Only the recording updates of my dicter phone, Shekhar's voice, and occasionally mine make their presence felt. Today is my first session with him to gather information for his biography.

The problem with writing a biography is, you, at times, start behaving as if it is your own life. You tend to filter moments and events through your own perspective. I have already started visualizing a young boy and a pretty girl, walking hand in hand through sunshine and rain. When the visual ruptures, it feels like a personal loss.

Shekhar nods his head. 'I didn't,' he states.

'What does that mean?' I ask, astonished.

'At twenty-four, I was looking for resources to invest. It was not a time for returns. But yes, I was attracted,' Shekhar says bluntly. 'Love takes time!'

Bewildered and even slightly hurt with his ruthless confession, I wish that this man had *some* romantic bone in his body. But before I am done abusing him in my silent monologue, Shekhar talks again and I am forced to concentrate.

'She was my student first, then a partner in my vision, a pleasant habit soon after; a lover only lately.'

I do have a hunch of what Shekhar is getting at. I have followed him closely in the last few months at Manhattan, though he did everything possible to cast me off. I throw a passing glance at the dark, deserted room in the corner, which, till yesterday was abuzz with commotion. Today it looks haunted, telling the story of its own fall. The image of a vibrant, fiery woman teases my memories. I had warned her about this day when she would be reduced to a mere image, conjoined with that of a vacant room she once frequented happily, but her aggression was way too ahead of logic.

I look back at Shekhar for more.

'Little did Manasi know that the dance she meant and the dance I was ambitious about, belonged to two different worlds. Her days post marriage were ones of rigorous training so that she caught up with my expertise at the earliest. Those days were anything but romantic, very much disconnected from what she had fantasized. But I needed a partner, not a disciple.'

Shekhar throws his head backwards, allowing it to rest on the back of his chair.

'I thought my life was a script pre-approved by myself. I had worked very hard to reach a stage where the things I wanted could be made possible. Life, though, has its own unpredictable ways to prove the best-laid plans wrong. And when it does so, people break, perish and rebuild; the new person who looks back at them from the mirror is someone they faintly recognize but never quite knew existed. In the process, the fundamental foundation of their being gets shaken for a lifetime.'

5

On the Arabian Shore

MANASI
Mumbai, 2015

Half-trained feet thump the floor in sync. As I walk down the staircase of our house in Mumbai, I can identify the beat going off-gear at times. Ali is helping the students to correct some postures. At a distance, Sunanda sits on the ground, staring in awe. I nudge her gently. 'What's brewing?'

'Nothing Akka.*' She is embarrassed. 'Nothing of that sort.'

I wink at her. 'I don't care about this sort or that sort. But Varanya might kill you.'

'No Akka,' Sunanda asserts. 'Ali resembles Anna so much.** The way he talks and teaches, looks like they are brothers.'

I smile at the girl's innocent adulation. Everyone here loves Shekhar. As much as Ali's resemblance to Shekhar in behaviour and pedagogy feels flattering, I would have been happier if Ali could come up with a distinct style of his own. But I cannot

---

*Akka: Tamil term for elder sister
**Anna: Tamil term for elder brother

blame the boy. Mirroring Shekhar comes naturally to all of us, even me. It is difficult to think beyond him.

I look at Ali again. 'They are brothers, Sandy; just that it's not by blood.'

Sandy gets up and follows me into the kitchen. 'You know, Akka, he has received so many scholarships under the sports quota. He has a trunk full of awards under his bed for the football matches he has won. Varanya was showing them to us the other day, until Ali stormed in, closed the box shut and threw us out.'

That too, he shares with Shekhar. The detachment from accolades. I don't say this; just sigh.

Ali displays some postures and asks the students to replicate. They bend and stretch to copy him, and quickly realize that the postures are not as easy as they look. They try individually and collapse. Ali helps each of them master it in turn. I smile at his patience.

'Anna says, nothing is personal in art. You have to develop that team spirit. Commit yourselves to the joint goals of the group. Always remember, guys, nothing or no one is ever bigger than the upcoming performance. *Sēānam'muteādyamunganana*!*'

Ali stops to drink water.

Just then, a voice from behind calls out, 'Foul, Ali bhai!'

Ali chokes on the water. I peep out of the kitchen to find Siddharth standing there with eyes half-closed like some ancient saint. That boy and his antics!

'According to the rules of Kala Mandir, which houses

---

*Sēānam'muteādyamunganana: 'The show is our first priority' in Malayalam students from different areas of the country, we are bound by a promise to prevent regional groupism.' I hear him talk loudly like a sports commentator. 'Whoever speaks a different language, has to teach the language to others. Ali bhai has just spoken in Malayalam, and hence, he'll have to teach it to the group standing next to him. Else, I'll complain to Anna.'

Sid is all animation, both in expression and voice. Ali laughs and throws both his hands up in the air.

In the midst of this bantering, Shekhar enters swiftly, his phone glued to his ear, talking to someone in Tamil. There is pin-drop silence everywhere; no one utters a word. Shekhar finishes his conversation and looks around.

'What?'

I burst out laughing. The others join in. Shekhar looks shocked, till I explain that he has earned himself a penalty for breaking his own rule.

'You'll have to teach Tamil to this group of twelve standing with Ali!'

Shekhar covers his face with his palm, smiling sheepishly and shaking his head.

Next, he calls us to gather for the mid-week meeting in a room at the rearmost corner of the bungalow, putting to end our lethargic, early-morning chit-chat.

In one such meeting two years back, we were discussing costumes for a show planned for a few months ahead. We were about to stage 'Lasya Ranjini', a composition featuring the beauty of the Karanas—a unique body vocabulary interspersed with extensive combinations of leg movements and dynamic arm movements. The term Lasya, in the context of Hindu mythology, describes the dance performed by Goddess Parvati. It expresses happiness and is filled with grace and beauty. She is believed to have danced the Lasya in response to the male energy of the cosmic dance of Tandava performed by Lord Shiva. In a literal sense, Lasya means beauty, happiness and grace. Many in the group had opined that costumes should have bright positive colours like orange, bright yellow or royal blue and debated over their choices.

When the discussion on costumes had just started, I had quietly written inside my writing pad, 'black'.

Shekhar loves his black costume in silk with strong red and golden borders; he accessorizes himself with a gold-plated brass belt on his waist. Its weight could restrict the movements of WWE champions, but Shekhar carries it with aplomb.

All morning, I simply sat witnessing the team discussing their logic with randomly picked colours, then going back to the philosophy of the composition to identify which colour justified it best, with everyone finally agreeing upon black.

Maybe after seventeen years husbands become predictable. Or maybe, wives get smarter.

Honestly, Shekhar is way ahead of the team in his planning. Each time his decision is already made. He only helps others to reach his vision through thorough brainstorming. With absolute command on himself and others, Shekhar monitors the spread of his life down to the last minute detail.

I often wonder, what is the bigger strength of my husband? The breathtaking performer that he is, or the people skills with which he manages his team, or his capacity to control minds so skilfully that they merge with his!

This morning, Shekhar may have caught my attention drifting. After the death of my father last year, he has grown more protective. Just before leaving the hall, he suddenly comes very close, holds me softly by the waist, brushes his mouth against my forehead, and disappears. Taken aback by the suddenness with which he comes and withdraws, I look around to find if anyone has been watching us. I place a hand on my shoulder and elbow, where I can still feel Shekhar's tender touch.

∽

Strong winds blow aside the window curtains, as the evening progresses towards night. He kisses me slowly, exploring my neck and nape. Our heavy breathing in the silence of the night feels like a storm somewhere. The dim light from the street lamps outside illuminates just as much as they should at this unprecedented hour of intimacy.

Meekly, I try to push him away. 'Let me go. I'm feeling cold. Got to shut the windows.'

Shekhar's eyes narrow at me. He holds me tighter, as if he hadn't heard a word of what I said. 'You made fun of me this morning. Face the consequences.'

I reason with him. 'You made the rule; so follow it now.'

But when has reason ever been able to stand up against desire? I place my hands around Shekhar's neck.

Shekhar draws closer. 'Shut up!' he whispers. 'I don't have the time to teach them Tamil.'

I grin and cuddle against him, trying to feel his warmth. Shekhar looks intently at my face. Suddenly, he raises my head to face him.

'Why did you go to the orphanage?' he asks.

Caught completely unaware, I hesitate. 'Jacob Sir told you?' Shekhar doesn't answer; just stares. The playful romantic mood of the evening has suddenly dissipated, as if it was never there.

My voice feels unsteady; words jumble inside my throat, before spilling out all at once. 'You never talk about your childhood, or the orphanage; not even in a careless unrestrained moment. But you own those days much more than your success, or even me.'

Shekhar doesn't say anything; slowly he loosens his hold on me. I hug him by the waist as tight as I can. 'Did I hurt you?'

Shekhar smiles. 'No; just made me a little conscious maybe!' He holds my hand and brings it to his chest.

The quiet between us feels depressing. Shekhar never tells me, but the loneliness and unbelonging of his orphanage days still haunt him. I have felt it in his unrelenting silence over anything that has to do with his past. Probably that is why he goes back to Thiruvananthapuram. To check if there is indeed something he can do to change that. The fear of an uncertain future triggered by the memories of a burdened past still chases him like a cynical tormentor.

And he is too reserved, too stoic, to disclose all of this to anyone. He snaps back dispassionately, 'My life is my responsibility, Manasi. I wouldn't trust anyone with either my emotions or obligations. The stakes are too high to risk. Leave my past alone. Don't ever try to revisit it. I will deal with it myself. Just that one dark corner of my life is not yours.'

What he has just said seems to negate all my devotion

during all these years. I am hurt, but stay quiet. He turns me to face him and brushes his nose against mine. I can't reciprocate.

'What?' he asks.

'Don't you feel it crushing, this necessity to be right every time?'

Shekhar draws back a little and looks at me. 'Now where did that come from?'

I throw myself into his arms and rest my head on his chest. 'At times I feel you aren't living a life. You just ruthlessly follow your plan; your own self-imposed expectations of flawlessness. That's scary.'

Shekhar laughs aloud. He brings his mouth very close to mine and whispers in a way that his voice seems to tickle my skin.

'I do make mistakes, Manasi. No one is perfect. Just like I fell prey to my own rule this morning. It happens all the time. But I have reached a stage where they call my mistakes an experiment; or maybe they just choose to ignore them.'

I don't answer. His warmth is spreading across my body and mind; I don't want anything to come between us. Shekhar takes a deep breath and touches the side of my face with his.

'Do you mean to say that you never had any complaint against me, Manasi?'

He looks at me, his gaze so intense that I fumble. Shekhar smiles affectionately, and answers his own question. 'You did; but never said it loud. You love to think that I am right. Or maybe you love to watch me be dominating. The same happens with others. They love me more than they love their complaints against me. And trust me, a love like that is very difficult to achieve.'

Shekhar goes back to exploring my body, rendering me absolutely powerless to utter a single word further.

∽

The day begins early for Shekhar. At 4 a.m. every day, he sits up on his bed, back erect and knees folded, for fifteen minutes of meditation. He manages to keep himself thought-free and concentrates only on his breathing. He takes time to inhale, focusing on drawing in air and exhaling it, lips tightly shut. He feels the air touching his lungs. He keeps it that way for three counts and exhales slowly. And repeats.

This exercise ends with a prolonged submission to Lord Shiva. With his knees bent in the earlier position he lowers the upper half of his body to touch the bed with his forehead, his joined palms stretched forward. He raises his upper body slowly without breaking the posture, keeps it erect for five seconds, and relaxes.

Almost immediately his mind starts reciting the Shiva Chalisa. He chants his way out of the room, to reach the balcony, thanks the gods for yet another beautiful day, prays for success and well-being, and then proceeds to take a bath. He wraps himself in a customary dhoti and enters the temple built at the centre of our bungalow, facing east. The camphor and incense sticks are already lit by then. He carries the smoke to all directions of the house. The ritual is declared open with the sound of bells.

I spring up on the bed with those bells dispelling all remnants of sleep. Late again! Shekhar has always been a morning person.

But I often stay up till late at night reading novels. So he doesn't wake me up at that unearthly hour when he leaves the bed. He takes strong offence though, every time I am late to the morning prayers. I pull myself into the bathroom, take a quick shower and rush to the temple. My hair and body are still wet, as are my clothes. Drops of water from my head trickle down my forehead and neck. Sheepishly I try to wipe them off first with my hands, then with the corner of my sari. Shekhar throws me a look of disapproval without stopping his chants. Quietly I take position beside him, lowering my head in front of the deities. From the corner of my eyes I glance at Shekhar and grin. It appears I would manage to escape his wrath today; he is in a good mood this morning.

Something vibrates to my left and I turn. Shekhar's phone, kept on the table beside the temple, blinks with a number from the US!

Who could possibly want to speak to Shekhar at this hour, and from the US, of all places?

6

The Voice

This is a two-storied mansion in Mumbai, where the ground floor is largely dedicated to the classes and rehearsals for Kala Mandir. There is a hall where meetings are held. A large kitchen is always active at one end of the house. The top floor accommodates Manasi and Shekhar's bedroom, their temple, Shekhar's study, and also some other rooms where outstation students who want to join the school can stay for a couple days till they find their feet in a new city. More often than not, if the guest rooms are vacant, someone or the other from the core group of Kala Mandir stays back.

On a usual day, some students would be practising the introductory steps of Bharatanatyam in one of the rooms downstairs. The beats produced by those bare feet on the ground creates a rhythm of its own, reverberating through all corners of the house. In another room, the shy, ever-smiling Emraan tunes the mridang as if he is born to play the instrument. Dhriti unmindfully plays the tanpura along with it, her attention wandering afar while her fingers mechanically do their job.

Today is a peaceful evening, with not much going on. Manasi has stepped out for shopping. Shekhar is reading a book in his study. He rests his head on the backrest of his chair. Such isolated, work-free evenings do not come to him too often. The apparent loneliness makes him conscious of his being, his life and the time that slips away making a fool of everyone who ambitiously tries to hold it back. The darkness outside feels like a complicated past; the unpredictable wind that pleasures his skin is as temporary as his many achievements.

Shekhar leaves his chair to stand in front of a garlanded photograph hanging from the wall. My photograph!

I may have left my mortal form a year ago, but somewhere in the subconscious of my son-in-law, I still exist. I happened to be a partial comfort provided by destiny to fill a huge vacuum in his life. Even after my death, Shekhar did not let loose of his hold on me. Desperately, he still clings on and tries to talk his heart out every time he has something to share. In fact, ever since I ceased to exist, Shekhar often discusses topics which he never touched upon when I breathed. Perhaps in front of the photograph, the questions are his, so are the responses; conversations are his, so are the reactions. Most of the time what Shekhar hears against his concerns today are words that I may have said in the past. The boy reiterates them in his brain. He imagines I am still there with him, questioning or morally supporting him in a way his biological father should have.

This evening Shekhar wants to reach out to his emotional shelter once again.

'Baba, you left too early. I still need you so much in life.' He touches the photograph. I smile.

'Everyone has to go one day or the other; I wouldn't have survived that long with diabetes had you not forced those healthy habits on me!'

Shekhar too smiles at the memory. Some memories cross his mind.

After prolonged persuasion he managed to convince me to adopt a vegetarian diet. He cajoled me to go out for early morning jogs. Shekhar would get ready within minutes in his track pants and sweatshirt; I would take time to choose the perfect shawl that matches my dhoti-kurta at five in the morning. Shekhar ran gracefully and fast, until sweat poured down his face and body. He would stop to look behind; he'd find me walking far behind with quick steps, responding to all the passers-by greeting me 'Nomoshkar, Thakur Moshai.' Shekhar would nod his head and run again.

I interrupt his reverie, telling him gently, 'But I left my most precious possession with you, son. My daughter, Manasi.'

Shekhar leans against the wall, supporting his head backwards.

'Manasi can't be your replacement, Baba. I still have a past to deal with, a future to build. I am not yet done with you.'

I am silent. Shekhar paces the room watching the other photographs, most of which are reflections of successful performances. I walk with him. He touches some of the photographs. 'You know Baba, Manasi finds it strange that people love me unconditionally. But why should they not? I am stylish, handsome, resourceful, knowledgeable and an absolute perfectionist with regard to my work. I am also quite protective towards my people. One or more of these traits always work to arouse interest and gather a following.'

Shekhar smiles, but the smile disappears as something in him prompts a response, probably what he had heard me saying many a times.

'You are also strangely disconnected, son.'

Shekhar repeats the same words that he always has for such an allegation. 'I have to be, Baba. Every journey is personal and lonely; every individual is all by himself. I have learnt to do things myself, without any support from anyone. I broke my way through so many obstacles. I can't be different today.'

He looks pensive. I say, after a pause, 'Hasn't Manasi supported you adequately?'

Shekhar takes a deep breath. 'She has. Her company is the biggest luxury of my life. She has been with me right from the time when I was no one, and she has never let me down.'

He is lost in his own world when the front door clicks open. The sleepy ground floor is suddenly active. Manasi has returned with a bunch of others. Shekhar's melancholy dissipates in the sudden hustle and bustle. He picks up the book he had been reading to keep it back on the rack, when Ali flings open the door and shouts, 'Anna, come soon. You are on TV! It's the interview from last week.'

Before Shekhar utters a word, he is gone.

Shekhar frowns. Why this excitement over an interview, he wonders. Not that he doesn't know why. His wife shares this excitement with his troupe, even encouraging their madness.

He makes a face.

'When will they learn to be indifferent about things like these?' he wonders aloud.

Shekhar's background has taught him there's nothing that is 'his', other than he himself. He is thus indifferent to the adulation of people. Past laurels mean nothing to him. But my daughter cannot, or will not, be as indifferent.

7

The Evening, Far Away

VATSALA PANDIT
Manhattan, 2015

After some visuals of their rehearsals, living room, etc., the camera focuses on the pretty young anchor of the news channel. She introduces the guest of the day.

The anchor: *Raj Shekhar Subramanian says he doesn't delegate anything completely. He likes to keep a keen watch on everything that he is involved in. His dance group, Kala Mandir, was not formed in a day. He keeps strict vigil on whoever is a part of his dance team, not only how well they dance but also the habits, tastes and choices that they make. He believes Bharatanatyam is a prayer; it is his way of worshipping the almighty; and one wrong priest can spoil his rituals. So here we are, in the courtyard of one of the world's most renowned schools of Bharatanatyam, talking to the Master himself.*

She turns to her right; the screen shows the Dancer sitting in his study.

My heart skips a beat. I sit up on my bed and put aside the

bowl of cereal I had been munching. He looks freshly bathed, with a white sandalwood mark on that broad forehead, a clichéd outfit—white t-shirt over blue jeans—and lots of red-yellow threads wrapped around his right wrist. No watch. He could have at least thrown a scarf around his neck!

I try to see more, as much as is possible through the restricted rectangular screen. The room has a book rack, a large window, and photographs of old shows, all of which I recognize even though they aren't exactly in focus.

Anchor: *Mr Subramanian, every Bharatanatyam enthusiast wants to join Kala Mandir. So what are the entry criteria here?*

Shekhar: *There is a very crucial question that I ask every candidate who aspires to be a part of my team—'How serious are you about Bharatanatyam?' I'll not allow anyone to join here for frivolous purposes; just to mention it on their CV. Only those who have genuine love for the art can join me. They must come to me to learn, not just to flaunt superficial skills and impress their schools during annual functions. My mentorship will not be exploited as a status symbol. I talk to the students and their parents myself before they are inducted to ensure that my rules are properly explained and agreed upon. So far I haven't made a wrong choice.*

He never asked *me* that! I wish he had. I have been learning the dance form from his old performances. In Manhattan, an amateurish Bharatanatyam dancer who doesn't even have any formal training would be called a lunatic if she updates her CV boasting she is an Indian classical dancer. But yes, I am an art-lover. Even if I don't mention it in my credentials, it is a defining factor of my existence. I can't underplay it, neither can any Raj Shekhar Subramanian deny it.

I almost start sulking. But the next question pulls me back to attention.

Anchor: *How is life within your academy?*

Shekhar: *Once inducted, everyone gets a diet chart prescribed to them by my nutritionist. It is obligatory for students to follow it. Along with learning Bharatanatyam, my students are known for their discipline and professionalism. They are not allowed to be late for the classes. They have a list of activities throughout the day and they are required to follow this schedule strictly. I make it clear to everyone that even a physical art like Bharatanatyam requires academic brilliance; hence, no one can neglect their studies excusing themselves for their devotion for dance.*

Huh! Sadist of the highest order. Discipline, my foot. The word is used only by frustrated oldies to keep others from having fun. Take a look around, man! You will find the world freaking out, dancing and enjoying their lives. And here this loner talks about caging human beings into following his definition of order and perfection. Get a life! You are so much in need of it.

Anchor: *And we have heard that you often don't charge your students for teaching them.*

Shekhar: *I don't charge those who come from modest backgrounds. Others, I do. But students aren't my business. I earn from my shows and other engagements. Students are my investments, not returns. The money they pay goes back into the funds of the academy. Once they learn the art, they would help me perform at important places and that's my ultimate revenue model. Even when I had started* *off with the academy years back, I maintained that money is not what I demand; my only expectation from students is sincerity and love for the art.*

This again touches my heart. This man could mint money just by giving his name to well-funded initiatives. He could declare that any kind of association with him would come at the price of a small fortune. But he takes the position that students aren't his investments. Bad entrepreneurial decision, but an artiste always picks up strange emotional ways to respect himself. You can't help developing a soft spot for such a man.

Anchor: *Tell us something about your mentorship extraordinaire. Your students are considered extremely well-behaved and intelligent by their academic guides. Teachers in schools and colleges compliment the parents for their child's maturity and focus in academics, sports and other extracurricular activities.*

Shekhar: *You need to involve the youth in constructive things. And introduce to them the joy of pursuing it. Don't show them rewards of money or recognition or appreciation. Talk to them about happiness, about fulfilment, about beauty. Motivation then comes from within and they don't depend on external rewards. If the youth trusts you and takes a step forward to walk with you, never cheat them. I give the best to my students. And they are happy to be with me. If you introduce beauty to the youth, they will stay away from nasty things and habits because their system instinctively rejects them. Every student of mine aspires to be with me on the stage. Because they appreciate the beauty that Raj Shekhar Subramanian translates on stage.*

True that. I aspire to be with him on stage.

This one sentence overpowers my senses. Everything else he utters after this passively enters my system. My eyes grow bright and large, measuring the possibility of truth in that dream. I just have to make it happen. I have to be right there, some day, on the stage with the arrogant Indian Dancer. Then I shall display my charm, mesmerizing the audience like a royal bride, available for them to feast their eyes on but well beyond their reach. I can be touched only by the one who sits today far away, in his own aloof dispassion towards anything that connects him to me. And there's only one magical spell which can break down the walls of that dispassion—Bharatanatyam.

It is time to dive into action.

I grab my mobile to call the Department of Cultural Affairs, New York. I am informed that 'Shekhar' would be updated about the recent developments within a day or two. Only some official formalities are getting sorted out.

I disconnect the phone and throw it up towards the ceiling. I whirl around, cheer in ecstasy and catch it just before it hits the ground. I have won the game again. I shake a can of beer vigorously before opening its mouth and allow the frothing liquid to spill all over, as if it were champagne. I hold it in style and sip, as I walk towards the balcony. The memory of that first interaction with Raj Shekhar Subramanian comes back, engulfing me from all directions. The hunk had ruthlessly broken my heart.

It is just a little over a year since then. The Indian Embassy in the US, in coordination with the DCA, is considering a proposal to invite him to set up a branch of his dance academy in the city of New York. I laugh and dance in euphoric madness.

This will defeat his vain ego, just like he crushed my aspirations some months ago.

He didn't know then that what I set my heart once, cannot be vanquished so mercilessly.

'See you in New York soon, Mr Subramanian,' I whisper to the image that has gone still on television.

8

The Call of Destiny

MANASI
Mumbai, 2015

The sea outside the window of our bungalow at Bandra is on high tide. The setting sun has cast its colours on the violent waves. As I sip my evening tea, my mind mulls over what Shekhar had said in his interview. He never says anything like 'I am lucky to be where I am', neither does he ever acknowledge God's blessings that he has received in abundance. Probably this is what you call confidence!

Before every show, Shekhar prepares a detailed diagram for his dancers. Each and every step is measured and calculated; each and every position discussed and re-discussed and modified. We never fuse any other form of dance in our offerings. But we don't put up a solo act either, like a traditional Bharatanatyam presentation. Our shows are no less than theatrical renditions.

One important area in which I help Shekhar is in selecting students for shows. He explains to me each moment of the three hours on the stage through his blueprints and picturesque descriptions of how he wants the performance to progress. I have largely taken over the process of deciding which dancer will play what role and would be positioned where. With all these years of practice and observation, I know every student's strengths and weaknesses minutely. So these days when I approach Shekhar with the names of selected dancers, I carry a list which mentions each character's actual and philosophical role as per the manuscript, demands of the character from the proposed dancer who would portray him or her, the dancer's job description for the show, their individual strengths and weaknesses, why he or she fits best into that character, and alternative dancers for all roles if Shekhar doesn't agree to my primary choice. Shekhar appreciates this systematic way of doing things. When he doesn't disagree with any of my choices and declares them final, I applaud myself for having learnt to successfully read his mind.

But I still feel butterflies in my stomach when asked to train the new students.

Initially when Shekhar spoke to the new joinees and took them through the theories of Bharatanatyam, I would quietly sit in a corner and listen to him. Or at times, when Shekhar invited me to exhibit some dance postures, I obliged. After a while though, Shekhar wanted me to take over this responsibility. I didn't say no, but requested Shekhar to stay away during my sessions. I felt conscious and intimidated by his presence.

I merely recited some passages in a crowd. Shekhar was always a live representation of each and every word he uttered. No two sessions of his were the same, because he spoke from the heart, enthralling his new students with his immense knowledge and the unique way he presented it. His passion was contagious.

At the end of my seventh lecture, I turned and found Shekhar standing in the doorway. Immediately, I stiffened. Shekhar smiled and left with a nod. Later, I asked Ali angrily why I wasn't informed about his presence, but he only laughed.

I can't blame him. Everyone in Shekhar's team knows what they are expected to do. It was foolish of me to believe that Shekhar would not keep a watch over me till he felt I am perfect at the job I had been assigned to do.

To put it more bluntly, Shekhar doesn't trust anyone.

One evening when he had come back tired and resigned, absolutely out of strength, I had confronted him.

'Why don't you just delegate some of the work that can happen without you? Why do you have to involve yourself in just about everything and return half-dead at the end of such gruelling days? Your possessiveness towards Kala Mandir is understandable but you have taken impossible responsibilities upon yourself, at the cost of your health. Just leave certain things to others and set yourself free,' I had said.

Shekhar just responded with, 'I can't.'

I know why. This is Shekhar's way of ensuring indispensability! He wants these few people to depend on him so much that they never leave him. He is a multitasker who does the work of ten people at a time to leave others eternally awestruck. In an odd way, the immense growth in his career is still slave to the economic and emotional deficiencies of his childhood.

Many winters have passed since then. But even today, while addressing students, I feel I am not even half as good as Shekhar. I still get those shivers down my spine if I spot him hanging around during my sessions. The only difference is, today I am in control of my emotions and verbal content. The peace I feel reflects in my training.

'The word Bharatanatyam is said to bring together bhavam, meaning expression; ragam, meaning music; thalam, meaning rhythm; and natyam, meaning dance. Bharatanatyam, is said to be the embodiment of music in visual form, a ceremony, and an act of devotion. There are three distinct elements to it: Nritta—the rhythmic dance movements, Natya—mime, or dance with a dramatic aspect, and Nritya—combination of Nritta and Natya. Bharatanatyam is considered to be a fire-dance—the mystic manifestation of the metaphysical element of fire in the human body. The movements of an authentic Bharatanatyam dancer resemble the movements of a dancing flame.'

I pause to sip some water, but stop as my eyes meet Shekhar's, leaning across the door with his arms crossed over his chest. His eyes sparkle with information. He has something to say which can't wait. Swiftly, I instruct the room to be darkened and the video of an old performance of Kala Mandir to be played for the students. I promise to come back and seek observation from the audience. In the next moment, I am standing next to Shekhar in his study.

Shekhar shows me an email that has come from the Department of Cultural Affairs, New York. The email invites Kala Mandir to start its operations in the city in collaboration with them.

Shekhar and his surprises… Or is this a shock?

I did know that Shekhar wants to spread the wings of Kala Mandir abroad and to bring dancers across geographies under the same roof. However, he had to keep his ambitions under check because international policies are not too friendly and most countries demanded that he take up their citizenship if he ever wanted to open a dance academy there. This disappointed him endlessly, but he never gave up.

I have seen him disappearing into his study for long meetings over Skype or calls, or go on tours without preamble, about which no one had ever questioned him. But none of us had the slightest clue that Shekhar is bringing upon us something so massive. He has taken one more step towards his destination!

I look up at him in bewilderment and realize that my reactions are being minutely observed. Before I say something, I am handed another email. This one suggests that Kala Mandir opens the doors of their New York branch with an inaugural show, which would be a charity event in collaboration with the United Nations. The scheduled date for this is barely eight months away.

I can sense heat building around my ears. Eight months and a little more. This is going to be difficult. I look at Shekhar with a frown. His eyes say there is more in store.

'I will have to leave for New York to set up the New York chapter of Kala Mandir. There's a lot of work to be done to get it rolling and some deals have to be made. I need to sign a co-ownership agreement with the Department of Cultural Affairs and the US Government, and the process would require some high-level meetings that won't end in a few hours. Hence, what we put up on stage eight months from now will be conceptualized and choreographed by you.' He comes closer and puts a hand on my shoulder. 'I need you to do this.'

My throat feels dry like a sunburnt desert as Shekhar finishes his last sentence. My hands are shaking; perhaps it is both excitement and anxiety. I reach out for Shekhar's glass and gulp down the water in it. By the time I gather the strength to speak again, Shekhar is gone.

Scared and lonely I look around searching for Shekhar, knowing pretty well that he isn't there anywhere waiting for me. A million doubts thunder inside my brain. Why did he have to do this all of a sudden, without even giving me enough time to absorb, understand and react? But he has already drawn the line of conclusion, leaving no scope of altering what he has just decreed. Quietly, I go back to class and resume the Induction Programme.

Thoughts still race in my mind. Planning and choreographing an act, deciding a theme, managing the dancers, orchestrating an entire group, sitting with musicians, visualizing the act inch by inch before it is finally staged, and all of these in the absence of Shekhar! I close my eyes once again, in denial. Shekhar's habit of policing everyone around suddenly feels most reassuring. But just when I need him to tell me that everything will be fine, he is nowhere.

Back in my bedroom, the silence feels scary, only to be interrupted by the sound of turbulent waves fretting outside the window.

Shekhar returns late at night. I am still upset and keep all verbal exchanges to a bare minimum. Shekhar has transformed a naïve girl from South Kolkata to a passionate Bharatanatyam dancer, but he hasn't taught me how to say no to his insane expectations. The more I think of it, more confusing it gets.

After dinner, Shekhar prepares coffee and sits beside me. I refuse to look at him in the eye; he keeps his glued on me.

An untamed restlessness builds inside me whenever Shekhar does this. My entire personality surrenders to him irrespective of how I feel about his unpredictable demands. The man never asks for my views. But I melt inside when he looks at me like he is doing tonight. My last attempt at retreat with a terse 'Good night, Shekhar,' falls flat as he is already behind me, standing very close and breathing down on my neck.

Moments pass like hours.

I can feel Shekhar's strong masculine fragrance engulfing so delicately that our bodies would touch if I move by half an inch. There are explosions within me. The ground seems to shake beneath my feet, as Shekhar touches my shoulders and brushes through my hair from behind, taking a deep breath. For a while I am completely numb. When I regain my senses, Shekhar's mouth is hungrily placed over mine. His unrelenting touch strokes and caresses my trembling lips, arousing passion and filling me with an insecure longing. My despair seems to evaporate within this bottomless desire.

Somehow it feels as if Shekhar is not just making love, he is communicating something. He is telling me how stressed he is at the moment; how orphaned he feels once again when I choose silence to combat his cold-blooded verdicts. I can read in the language of his body an urge, a desperation, to pull me out of my cynical, sombre mood and get me to walk with him steadily like I always do.

Slowly I open my eyes to look at him.

Some fine lines on the large forehead, patches of grey around the ears, a stiff jaw. For a fleeting second Shekhar too opens his eyes to look back at me, his probing vision seeking a million clarifications, before he buries his face back into my shoulder.

Is Shekhar trying to test my perseverance tonight?

This is the last question that erupts in mind before I lose my senses to his warmth spreading generously across my bare back.

Just when I have submitted myself completely, Shekhar pulls back. Softly he touches me but refuses to indulge any further. With a subtle roguishness, unusual in him, Shekhar is wordlessly calling upon me to come ahead and take charge, or remain fallen, unfulfilled.

In the darkness of the room, broken only by the faint lights from the window, I see another side of Shekhar. The man who is trying to disconnect from everything that is his and preparing himself for a lonely journey yet again to unlearn and relearn, to rebuild, to open himself to the insecurities of being judged right from the beginning. A fresh start. And Shekhar wants reassurance from his very first student, as if no one else exists and any opposition from her can crush his world.

Like a possessed serpent that dances tirelessly to the tunes of her charmer, I draw closer to him, attacking his withdrawal with a vengeance. The purpose that Shekhar is living for has started playing its bohemian music all over again, and I am drawn by the same inexplicable pull I had felt all those years ago, when he spoke to me for the first time.

I was with him then, and I will be with him now. Nothing has changed.

As my tenderness comes in contact with Shekhar, it conveys a haste to overcome all resistance that had clouded my mind few hours ago. At the pinnacle of pleasure, we unite again to start the same journey afresh. When Shekhar finally lowers his exhausted body next to mine, I feel my head no longer heavy with an impending tension. My apprehensions still keep me awake till the wee hours of the morning, though, while the husband rests himself peacefully on my chest and sleeps like a baby.

9

The Voice

The car speeds through the surprisingly empty roads of Mumbai. Buildings, trees and roads get left behind at an increasing pace. Lost in thoughts, Shekhar feels the same happening in his own life.

Manasi looked nervous and shaken. Will she be able to pull this off? Would this backfire? Well, even the possibility of such a situation is not something he can afford to accommodate.

He sits up.

It has to work out. No space for ifs and buts.

I intervene to soothe his restless, burdened heart. Shekhar begins talking to me, 'Won't you congratulate me, Baba?'

There is complete silence everywhere. Shekhar closes his eyes, lets his head fall back for support on the rear seat of the car, to submit to the old man from a not-so-distant past.

'Baba, you always possessed a strange capacity to trust the people around you. A quality which I never had. You trusted that your daughter is in safe hands. As long as you lived, I spent a lot of time with you while preparing for each new show so that your positivity rubs off on me. Your affectionate presence gave me so much reassurance, something as an orphan I never experienced in childhood.'

My voice resonates within his brain. 'I'll pray for your success, son. My prayers for you haven't perished with me.'

'Manasi seemed scared, Baba. I need her to take up this assignment with confidence. It's all in the attitude. Why isn't she prepared to face such sudden developments as and when they come? Why does she still need an introductory phase? Those are for newbies.'

'Women are an ocean of strength, my son. It is just that they are made to grow up with the belief that they are weak. I'm sure my daughter won't disappoint you,' I assure him.

Some dark clouds hover inside Shekhar's brain, casting vague shadows. 'Baba, I am taking a big risk in attempting this. Performing worldwide and getting accolades doesn't require life-altering investments. But setting up another India with its purest culture in a foreign country might take my reputation with it, if it fails.'

'What was the urgency to establish yourself abroad, my son? You could have spread Kala Mandir within other cities in India,' I say.

Shekhar shakes his head vigorously in disagreement. 'Any art form is like a culture or a civilization, Baba. It needs to expand and increase its outreach if it has to grow and sustain.' He pauses, his eyes searching for something abstract in the sunlit clouds outside.

'I don't need to reach out to other cities in India. People from all over the country come to me anyway. Sometimes I even have to sort out their schooling, boarding and lodging to support their passion towards Bharatnatyam and me. I want to reach out and be more accessible, even outside India, to NRIs and foreigners. There has to be an amalgamation of creative inputs and the cultural exchange will only enhance the richness of our craft. I need to learn and explore more, to avoid becoming redundant.'

I assure him once again, 'Then pursue your karma, son, and everything else will follow. Even if the eventual outcome fails to meet your expectations, you will not be without some gain. At the end of the day, something, whatever it be, will be yours.'

10

The Face of Resistance

RAJ SHEKHAR SUBRAMANIAN
Mumbai to Manhattan, 2015

The journey from Mumbai to New York is a long one. I wait at the VIP lounge after the security check at the airport. My phone beeps. It is Tim Smith, Chairperson of the Department of Cultural Affairs (DCA) in the USA.

'Congratulations, Shekhar. You must be a happy man now,' Tim says.

I smile. 'Thanks, Tim. New York is finally mine.'

Tim laughs at the other end of the phone. 'Shekhar, we never had any qualms about going ahead with your proposal. We were just concerned about its takers in this market. People love to experience new things, but they may not wish to practise them.'

'Leave it to me to make things happen. I can make people crave to live the life of Raj Shekhar Subramanian. They can't, till they embrace Bharatanatyam. It's a cakewalk for me, as long as you silly people don't come in between,' I think silently. Aloud, I can't stop myself from asking, 'What convinced you finally, Tim, to decide in my favour? I can't quite trust that you invested in a market research survey.'

Tim's response takes me by surprise.

'We did, but not before we had sufficient reasons to invest our time and money. That report is not the only catalyst that worked.' He pauses. 'There's this young lady, an advertising professional of sorts, who had submitted applications after applications to the DCA, requesting the authorities to bring your dance academy to New York for the cultural enrichment of local performers. Every time, the number of signatures in her applications increased more than double. No one knows how she managed to gather so many enthusiasts interested in learning Bharatanatyam, that too from no one else but you, Shekhar. She is known to have conducted many road shows and events that helped in spreading awareness; she is also running some fantastic social media campaigns. This lady arranged for open-air promotional shows right outside the gate of the Embassy. She gathered people, showed them your YouTube videos, spoke about the history and benefits of pursuing the ancient art, and so on. Her dedication aroused interest in a considerable number of people, and the Embassy was forced to give the proposition a serious thought.'

I fall silent. My jaw tightens, as anger seethes through my veins. Grimly, I just thank him once again before hanging up.

I hear my boarding call and get up from my seat.

The words of Tim Smith linger, akin to a brazenly stubborn insect which won't bite, but will still buzz so irritatingly that it can drive you insane.

I remember this girl. The one who told me a year ago that one day she will make me come to Manhattan and teach her

Bharatanatyam. This is a welcome step towards my goal, but I can't feel happiness any longer. No one in my world is brave enough to work against my wishes. I require no one's help to get what I want. I cannot savour my success, knowing it is due to someone else's efforts, not solely mine. This girl is walking towards me, unheeding of the fact that I don't quite appreciate her existence anywhere close to my world.

To brush off these random disturbing thoughts, I pick up the file that DCA had mailed to keep myself updated on the work that has already been processed.

I study the papers minutely and make notes on the issues which still need to be addressed. They have arranged meetings with three business tycoons who are coming in as sponsors. Then there are the venture capitalists I am supposed to meet in a day or two. The first thing I need to focus on now is an aggressive marketing plan to rope in a massive audience for the inaugural show. I have to remain available to the national media in person to sound out my strategies and specific commitments towards my American students. A press conference will follow just a day after I land.

Before walking in through the security check point, I had instructed Manasi to prepare a draft of the initial vision of her act as soon as possible and mail it across to me so that I can start preparations at my end.

A range of emotions course through my mind as I close my eyes to think of her sultry face. I have thrust too much upon her all of a sudden. Obviously, I wouldn't leave everything to her. I would move strings to orchestrate progressions. The only assurance I needed from Manasi is to handle my physical absence. It would be difficult to hold the show together, but not impossible.

This is not the first time that I have chosen to pursue a scary target. My history reflects that pattern in abundance.

Manasi looked nervous and sad at the airport. The depression, though, was about her impending separation from me.

I set aside the papers for a moment. Usually I don't encourage these emotions to overpower me. Not openly at least. One moment of weakness can weaken my resolve and take me several steps backwards. I don't have the luxury for that.

I open the file again and flip through some papers. One paper carries the names of volunteers. I take it out and scan it with a frown. One of the chief volunteers is Vatsala Pandit.

The back of my head hits the stand of the seat as I move back in alarm and frustration.

Lord, don't do this to me. My dream-come-true moment can't be ruined by the ill-humoured charity of some obsessed female. I am in a dilemma—I want to go ahead and fulfill my ambitions and yet, a part of my brain also wants to dump the offer to defeat the desperation of this woman!

I close the file in disgust and throw it aside.

My achievements and failures are solely mine. At the end of my journey I shouldn't have anyone to thank, nor anyone to blame. I am my own chariot. I am the horse that gallops away to glory or falls to failure. I don't need a Vatsala Pandit to fulfill my dreams. But she has forced her way in nevertheless and I want to cast her off.

I feel bitter. Restlessly, I untie the seat belt and unbutton the top of my shirt, trying to get some fresh air.

The girl has chained me into a situation she knows I can't avoid. This is not the awe of a regular fan. There's more to it. Her giving isn't an act of generosity towards art. Bharatanatyam is my purest prayer. I can't allow such elements to touch and spoil what I have built with the dedication of a lifetime. Each time I think of her, my irritation multiplies. I will have to meet her now, despite my apprehensions, because she is one of the chief volunteers in this venture.

I wish I could avoid this.

Finally, I land at John F. Kennedy International Airport. Vatsala is among those who have been sent to receive me. I remain warm to the organizers, and ignore her completely. I greet everyone with a polite smile but refrain from acknowledging the venom that comes from a pair of eyes on my right.

11

The Intruder

VATSALA PANDIT
Manhattan, 2015

My eyes burn; my throat feels heavy with the insult.

Is he faking it or does he just like playing pricey? I badly want to reach out to him, hold him by his shoulders and shake him hard, so that he wakes up to me and the reality. It is with my assistance that his dance academy is about to come up in Manhattan. Obviously I can't follow my instincts, which disturb me more than this man's unnerving misbehaviour. Shekhar, though, remains oblivious to my state of mind, or so he shows.

It is only in the evening, when he is personally meeting those who will be associated with Kala Mandir's New York chapter, that he looks at me. He keeps his eyes steady and unblinking for a good ten seconds, till he moves on to the next person.

I have no idea how I must interpret this brief stare. It is certainly not a kind, pleasant gaze. He doesn't smile, speak or exchange any pleasantries, turning my excitement into pensive deprivation. I had expected, if not generous thanks, at least a word of appreciation, as I had put in my blood, sweat and tears for this moment.

That dark face, though, is impassive.

After standing like a stone for a while, I leave the venue. A friend, who came along with me, pats my back attempting to calm me down. I push her away.

'What does he think of himself? Why should I have to bear the brunt of this cruel, ill-mannered crackpot?' I blabber with angst. Wrath bubbles inside my brain like a turbulent river; just that the rock it wants to crash against is undeterred and distant.

A wave of grief sweeps through me. 'I was so excited to meet him,' I admit sadly.

The friend winks and says, 'But he isn't.'

I flare up again. 'I won't let him get away with this. He'll not play these mind games with me for long.' I promise, and without a word more, I storm out of the venue.

It is drizzling outside; Manhattan is unusually windy. I walk down from Times Square till Chelsea market, grab a sandwich and coffee, and hurl curses at the guy serving it as he almost spills the coffee on my foot. The guy leaves with a grim face. He is mostly accustomed to my mood swings. He knows what happens when I have had a bad day. He walks a few steps ahead and looks back to check if I am fine. I devour the sandwich with large bites, chewing hastily and gulping down more at a time than what is usually considered decent. I throw the leftover morsels in the dustbin and leave the restaurant to walk further down till the Brooklyn Bridge, but not before I have left a more than reasonable tip on the table.

The breeze feels cold. I pull up the hood of my jacket. I come here often, skating along the Bridge to compete with some friends amidst shrill laughter and cursing each time one skater leaves another behind. But the Hudson River has probably never witnessed my melancholy. Neither has it ever found me standing alone at a corner, looking beyond the water, not reacting to its eternal ebb and flow.

My limbs feel weak. My clothes, wet from the drizzle, are not the only things that are uncomfortable and clumsy.

To whom do I explain that my fascination for Raj Shekhar Subramanian is not just an immature, randomly acquired crush? It is about his brain that reacts creatively every time the Carnatic music plays, and the sculpted body that postures so gracefully to enthral his audience. Those few seconds when he had looked at me with his unblinking gaze, I had felt him reaching out to the depth of my vulnerabilities; yet I could not look away till he left me, lonely and haunted amidst everyone else.

Late at night, I walk quickly back through the same path, straight to the VIP suite in the DCA guest house. This time no one stops me.

I knock on his door roughly, with all the pain accumulated at the tip of my finger, as if another painful sensation would counter the despair of the evening. I don't care that it is well past the time when I can reach out to someone with such a passing acquaintance. I just know that I have to convince the Dancer to teach me Bharatanatyam; come what may I have to go back with his 'yes'.

The door opens. His disconcerted eyes look shocked by the intrusion at this hour. I don't think much but just lash out with whatever words spill out of my mouth, gasping in rage and fighting back the disappointment that almost fills my eyes as tears.

12

The Secret Audience

BRIAN HERRETT
Manhattan, 2015

Only one other person besides Shekhar and Vatsala stands here attending this bizarre meeting. That's me.

I was in the elevator, on my way back after I met Shekhar for dinner. As the elevator touched the ground, a young sassy girl rushed in, almost pushing me aside, and hastily pressed the button to his floor without waiting for me to depart. I had seen her at the airport when I went to receive Shekhar, though not as an assigned representative of the DCA. She had been running around trying to get everything in place, very evidently a bundle of nerves. I lost sight of her once Shekhar from the security gate.

The possibility of this young tornado trying to meet Shekhar half an hour after midnight was good enough to tickle my curiosity. Standing behind her in the elevator, I found her half-drenched, though that did not seem to bother her.

What I gather from the brief exchange of words, standing in the enclosed terrace, isn't too encouraging. A focused artiste and an obsessive follower usually makes for a great scandal, only as long as one of them is not Raj Shekhar Subramanian!

For a while Shekhar can't believe that the girl is indeed standing at his door. He fights to keep his anger under wraps, the heat of his eyes ready to burn the girl's confidence to ashes. Yet, she doesn't seem to be the type to be intimidated.

'What brings you here?' Shekhar's voice is soft and curt. Her heated response comes quickly.

'I did try a reasonable path to reach you, but you did not value that. May I know what exactly makes you think that I am carrying my self-respect on my sleeves which you can kick into mud whenever you desire? Or is it because I came to you by myself, that you safely assume I am available for your bizarre temper tantrums?'

She leans on the corner of the open door as he stands blocking her way inside. She shows no interest in entering the room. Her audacity shocks me; perhaps even Shekhar.

I pray that the door isn't slammed shut on her.

Arms crossed across his chest, jaw clenched tight, veins on his forehead throbbing in fury, Shekhar stands in awkward silence.

'Speak up, girl. Don't waste time. He is waiting to hear from you,' I almost blurt out, but stop myself with professionally trained restraint.

She shakes her head, further messing up her already dishevelled hair. 'Let's sit in the lounge downstairs for fifteen minutes please; in fifteen minutes if I can't convince you of my purpose, then I will be gone forever. Take my word.'

I am highly amused. The girl seems crazy and this is getting interesting. Shekhar doesn't move an inch.

She waits for him to respond. When he doesn't, she shrugs.

'Teach me Bharatanatyam exclusively every day; choose your time and I'll be available. In three months flat, I'll be a better performer than the best student in your team. I bet you.'

It seems like her intellect has gone floating through the waves of the Hudson. I can't imagine what kind of person speaks with such impulsive pride, challenging years of perseverance and skill with such demonic resolve. She possesses simultaneously the boldness of a child and the desperation of the devil. One part of me wants to slap her in the face; the other wants to protect her.

Shekhar stares at her in cold silence. Then he softly utters, '3 a.m. tomorrow morning.'

The girl nods, adjusts her grip on the bag hanging across her back and walks off. Shekhar goes inside to stand on the balcony, watching her leave his premises.

Downstairs, she puts on her roller skates and flows like water from one end of the house to the other. Dangerously she goes down a few flights of stairs with the skates on and balances herself on the cement floor with professional ease. She breezes straight from left to right on one leg, lifting the other up in the air, hands stretched outwards like the blades of an aeroplane. As she reaches the boundary of the guest house, she lets the raised foot fall on the ground and whizzes out of the main gate.

From the corner of the building where I stand, I can see Shekhar. He lets out a grin watching the girl leave and sobers almost immediately, leaving me intrigued.

I have known this man for many years now. I can vouch that neither anger nor mirth comes very naturally to him. Who the hell is this woman who can get Shekhar enraged and amused, both at the same time?

13

The Black Goddess

MANASI
Mumbai, 2015

In Shekhar's study, I take off the garland from the frame and replace it with a new one. I place sandalwood paste on Baba's forehead from over the glass of the photograph, then bow down before him, seeking his blessings. This is the one ritual that Shekhar loves to do himself every morning. I do it only in his absence.

A large part of my childhood was spent in Chandannagore. Baba was posted in Bhilai in those days.

He did not wish to uproot me and my mother from Bengal. Rather, he envisaged that if his family stayed in Bengal, it would be easier for him to negotiate with SAIL and request for a transfer to Durgapur or at least Bokaro. But that didn't quite happen. His superiors in Bhilai were extremely happy with his hard work and sincerity and ensured his transfer never came through. Every time his transfer papers received a stay order. so, Baba would come to meet us three or four times a year.

Even from a distance, his efforts in bringing up his only

daughter never suffered or faltered. Right from the age of five, I received long letters from him. He wrote about everything that he would have spoken to me had he been near. Equally, he encouraged me to write back. In my immature handwriting I would talk about the first-floor balcony with a pond beneath, the ducks that played on the water, the kingfisher pair who were guest visitors, how I loved sitting there alone when everyone slept in the afternoon, the sunset from the terrace, the food my mother cooked, how I hated the milk she forced down my throat, and many other innocent problems and happiness, joys that captured and filled my little mind. Baba responded with his own thoughts and experiences that he felt mattered; in each of his letters he also pointed out the spelling mistakes and grammatical errors in my letters.

As we both grew, topics of letters touched upon literature, poetry, art, geography, philosophy and God. We discussed difficult subjects with remarkable ease. A new thought that appeared in our minds or the experience of reading a new book never felt complete till we shared it with each other.

In Baba's absence, I spent my days at my maternal uncle's place in Chandannagore. Located on the Hooghly River, Chandannagore is a small town and a former French colony, some 30 kilometres away from Kolkata. I loved walking along the famous Chandannagore strand, studded with lights and surrounded by lush green trees, enjoying the mild breeze and watching the small boats sailing on the river. Often, I would sit for hours on the beautifully decorated river bank until someone informed me that my family was looking around for me at home, and then I would run back.

What also attracted me was an imposing structure along the Hooghly, a meditation centre called Vivekananda Mandir.

When Baba retired, he came back to Kolkata and gathered the extended family of his brothers and first cousins to stay together in the house built by their grandfather in South Kolkata. He took up the priest's duties at the nearby Shiva temple, just like his father and forefathers had done. He took me with him so that I could understand the process. I was asked to play the conch shell in between his chants; long and smooth I played it with a steady rhythm and dragged it till I could hold my breath no more.

He was surprised though, that I did not share his devotion towards worshipping the deities. I would often be unmindful about arranging things for the puja and leave things half-done. Rather, I would be listening more attentively to the songs of a beggar woman seated on the lowest step on the temple, singing praises of Goddess Kali.

One day, Baba tried to talk to me about it. Affectionately he placed his hand on my head and tried to probe. 'Out of all the deities who do you like more, Manasi?'

'Kali. She spells power,' I replied immediately. 'I feel Kali is the true companion of Shiva. She destroys the inner evil. She cleans the world of wrongdoing and corruption. You worship Kali on amavasya* nights and by the time the rituals get over, it is morning. Don't you find that wonderful, Baba? The deity who leads you out from a black night to the bright morning?'

I paused to observe my father's reaction. He didn't look

---

*Amavasya: new moon night

upset or angry.

Baba had taken a deep breath and asked, 'So, do you worship Kali?'

'No, Baba. But I feel Shiva and Kali symbolize true companionship; the collective purpose of being and sharing a divine presence where their destinations and paths are the same.'

My father smiled. He may have seen that there was much more to this in his daughter's heart, but I couldn't gather my thoughts well enough to explain any further.

Baba reopened this discussion with me from time to time. Every time I stopped nervously beyond a point when words would fail and my heart ached because I was unable to articulate something important.

∽

Kali is the goddess associated with empowerment, or Shakti, the power of Shiva. Kala or kaal means black, signifying time and death. Shiva is called Kāla—the eternal time—and Kālī, his companion, is the Goddess of Death, her arms being Time and Change. She is often depicted as dark and violent, because her core purpose is the annihilation of evil forces. The Kalika Purana defines her as Adi Shakti, the fundamental power and Para Prakriti, meaning beyond nature. Kali's association with darkness stands in contrast to her consort, Shiva, who manifested after her in creation, and who symbolizes the rest of creation after Time was created. In supreme awareness of spiritual truth,* his body is covered by the white ashes of the cremation ground (śmaśāna in Sanskrit) where he meditates, and with which Kali is also associated, as śmaśāna-kālī or Shamshan-kali. In times of natural disasters she is invoked as the protective Raksha-kali.

In her most famous pose as Daksina-Kali, the Goddess is said to have drunk the blood of her victims on the battlefield, dancing with destructive vigour. Kalī idols are often seen standing on the body of Lord Shiva. They say, Shiva subdues her anger. She was about to destroy the universe when Shiva laid in her path, in order to stop her. In her fury, she failed to see Shiva, who lay among the corpses on the battlefield and stepped on his chest. Realizing that the Lord lied beneath her feet, her anger was pacified. The Devi Purana explains that Lord Shiva beneath her feet represents matter, as Kali is undoubtedly the primeval energy. The depiction of Kali on Shiva shows that without energy, matter lies dead!

I shut the book I had been consulting.

My fondness for Kali had started when I read the works of Ramkrishna Paramhansa and later, the complete works of Swami Vivekananda in my teens. Since then, whenever I went to the Dakshineswar temple in Kolkata with my mother, I felt awakened.

I adore the red hibiscus flower used compulsorily to worship the black Goddess. During sunset, I visualize two large bloodshot

---

*http://www.vedicupasanapeeth.org/kali-the-consort-of-shiva/

eyes opening slowly to look down at the earth. My soul reaches out to the divine as I join my hands and touch my forehead, standing on the terrace every evening, invoking the Goddess in my heart and submitting as a miniscule mortal embodiment to her supreme vastness.

In the meaning and representation of Kali, I find the most feminine purpose of a woman.

'Destroy everything that adds to your pride; in fact, destroy your pride. Rebuild and rediscover, as if you are no one and you never had anything. Cleanse your system. Let not the evil tempt you towards a mundane existence. Exist fearlessly, as if there is no tomorrow; because actually, there isn't one,' I remember the preacher at Vivekananda Mandir saying thus.

It is perhaps this fearlessness that lead me to instinctively marry a man who was going to pursue an uncertain career.

That evening I had smelt adventure in Shekhar's proposal. I saw no more than those tough features of his face. His jaw line as he spoke, the calm of his eyes, his half smiles and his tall build mesmerized me and filled my fantasies. I had waited there, in the room where we met, secretly exploring something mysteriously exceptional that he may have left behind after he was gone. I couldn't decipher what it was but I was convinced there was something because I could feel it very closely within my senses. Shekhar's confidence shone brighter than the vague life he had proposed. Not for once I felt that stability or security might be an issue with this man.

The Goddess however, did not leave me at that. Kali still visits my dreams often. Earlier, Baba would chide me for dancing with the dhaak, the holy beats of Goddess Durga. But every year during Durga Puja, when the dhaak played, I found it impossible to resist a strange call that urged me to match steps with the Goddess of my imagination. And this is the only secret that I kept away from my father, my husband and from the rest of the world. Not because I want to hide it, but because I don't know how to disclose something like this.

Now that I am preparing the script for our inaugural show at Manhattan, I will conceive a theme based on Kali. Kala Mandir has staged dance-dramas on Shiva and Shankara, and Durga and Parvati. But never on Kali.

May the Goddess who has forever haunted my consciousness, finally descend.

14

Mentor at Work

RAJ SHEKHAR SUBRAMANIAN
Manhattan, 2015

What an awkward, lingering pain this woman is! There must be a way to get rid of this madness, just that I can't figure out how. I hit the railing of the balcony with my fist and get back into the room to fall flat on the soft bed.

As much as I detest her, I had promised to make her my first student if Kala Mandir ever came to Manhattan. I can't go back on my word now. I don't want to admit this, but she has done a fantastic job here without any assurance of returns. But the moment I am good to her, she'll expect all kinds of privileges.

I am intrigued though, with her tendency to constantly talk targets. Last time it was about getting Kala Mandir to New York; today it is convincing me in fifteen minutes flat. And then declaring that she'll dance better than the best dancer in my troupe if I train her for three months!

For a long time, I have been tossing and turning on my bed. Deserted by sleep, those words echo in my brain—'In three months, I'll be a better performer than the best student in your team.'

The best in my team is my wife, Manasi! No one can ever be like her. I have given her a part of my soul, the meaning of my being, my solemn unforgiving pursuit of a lifetime. By taking upon this challenge, the girl has also challenged me to repeat my exclusive mentorship, something that I have given only to Manasi.

I am not sure what annoys me more. The fact that she has unknowingly equated herself with Manasi, who is my best and most prominent testimonial as a coach? Or that she dared to speak to me with such impertinence?

Fine, I'll train her if I have to, only to find out if there is one other soul on this earth, who can represent me with equal finesse as Manasi. I also want to know whether Vatsala's determination can ever defeat Manasi's dedication. If there's a fraction of truth in her challenge, then along with Manasi, my pride would also be defeated.

I leave the bed, pour some wine and open the laptop to dig out all possible information about Vatsala. I scroll through her social media profiles and other sites that mention her, reluctantly trying to don the shoes of a mentor yet again, preparing to tame a different brand of wildness.

Various updates across her social media accounts suggest myriad interests or disinterests. Born to a half-Indian father and a British mother, Vatsala Pandit shines bright as a match-winner in the local volleyball team. There are images of her performing difficult ballet postures. There are also rambling accounts of different occasions when her unsettled soul brought severe trouble upon her peers. She does not come across as apologetic or sympathetic to any of these people.

Vatsala works for an advertising agency and rehearses with her ballet group during the evenings. Her friends have poured out lavish praise for her ballet performances. They say she floats on the stage like a swan and can emote so convincingly that her audience goes back misty-eyed.

A post shows her arrested by cops for honking her bike's horn too loudly and incessantly in the middle of a calm residential neighbourhood, unheeding to the inconvenience caused to residents; when asked she said it was fun. Images of her posing shamelessly in handcuffs have been shared endlessly across social media platforms.

The wine at this sleepless hour feels good. It offers the patience I need right now.

A bald guy who is often at the receiving end of her sarcastic verbal jibes is probably her boss. Her friends opine that she hasn't yet lost the job because she is extremely good at her work. There are updates where she celebrates her stupid adventures, garnering both encouragement and warnings from her admirers. She mentions how she parked herself in front of schools and playgrounds on some days, painting anything from watches on wrists or moustaches on upper lips, to Satan's eyebrows or Princess Diana's necklace on the tender skins of the kids. Next day when parents came to complain, she was somewhere else committing some other nuisance, generally beyond the reach of those who wanted to mend her ways.

Even when she loses a volleyball match, her updates are replete with pride as if she has intentionally given up on a whim; images clicked at the moment capture her throwing pitiful glances at the winners. Once when she had been arrested again for a minor offence, it had come to light that she had planned it deliberately because the 'sergeant was cute'. She had a fling with him lasting two weeks, before moving on. Her followers mostly laughed and cheered; those who tried to caution her were subjected to tongue-lashing.

Many in the town must be nurturing a fond dream to bury her alive someday. I want to switch off the laptop and keep her restricted to the other end of the screen, which I would never visit again.

And then, her next post takes me by surprise.

Every weekend after the prayer services are over, she walks into the old age home adjacent to the local church carrying fruits, milk, clothes, books, DVDs and other gifts to cheer up the senior citizens banished from life by their fate. She believes that one day she would end up there too. It is just her way of bribing destiny.

Bharatanatyam is her latest obsession and so am I! Her profiles feature various updates on the dance form and its history, and there are several photographs and videos of me and my troupe performing.

Vatsala seems to be just the kind of pain people want to avoid, but she is equally a force that is difficult to resist.

The wine is beginning to take effect. I shut down my laptop and walk towards the balcony.

Some compromises are a part of the larger deal. Just when I thought I have grown beyond the control of compromises, Vatsala storms in. It's outrageous. She is the last person I would ever want to see as my student. The flickering disquiet refuses to let me respect the dedication she has already shown in her campaigns to bring Kala Mandir to New York. Her commitment and her personality make for an odd, unfathomable contradiction. It disturbs.

The moisture-laden breeze pierces through the skin to touch my nerves. I can feel it distancing my mind from this girl, as it goes back to the abode where my loved ones reside.

It isn't as if I haven't dealt with such elements in the past. Take Siddharth. He is almost a replica of Vatsala's desperate energies. He too would have grown up to be something close to this, had I not restrained his wildness right in the beginning.

These memories finally help me regain my calm.

The boy was multi-talented and he was on a spree to explore the world. Three times he fled his home in Delhi to reach my dance school; each time I sent him back with an attendant who dropped him to his house. The first time he ran away, he was only thirteen years old. He yelled, cried, fell at my feet and did all kinds of drama. He didn't want to go back to his Punjabi parents who took immense pride in their restaurant business and butter-blessed food. But I was not ready to hear out his stories. Finally, the boy managed to convince his parents. With a heavy heart, they succumbed to their 'foolish' son's love for 'some South Indian thing'.

Surprisingly, Sid did not carry the loud Delhi culture with him. He possessed aesthetic tastes and carried in his brain a distinct understanding of colours. Often, before and after our shows, Manasi found him sitting before a laptop loaded with strange software. He used those on the images of the performers to change the colours of their costumes and themes and compared the difference. During his idle hours, he would sit sketching the look of the dancers. He never showed those to me. Manasi had once got hold of the sketchbook and looked through the pages, unheeding of his protests. She told me that the boy had a masterful eye for detail, as his inputs were impactful in the shaping of various characters.

And I was also informed that Sid had been secretly interning with some renowned designer in Mumbai. Before Manasi came to know about it, I bumped into the designer at a social do. Back home, I instructed Varanya to discreetly keep an eye on Sid.

Sid is still the rebel in the team!

And Manasi.

Once in Delhi, in Sarojini Nagar market, I was away for fifteen minutes and she had started talking and laughing with a mentally challenged beggar. They both sat on the stairs of a Shani temple. Much to my horror and embarrassment, she was found playing with coins with the beggar woman, laughing every time her coin hit those of the opponent's. I was enraged by her impropriety.

And yet again, in Bangalore, I found her with schoolchildren, helping them to steal mangoes from someone else's tree. While crossing the lane in my car, I discovered her standing on the bonnet of some car parked on the side, holding high a kid with both hands while the mini demon was busy plucking mangoes and throwing them down for his friends to gather. Of course, I did not want to be seen at the mercy of my wife's whims begging her to step down, in public. I dialed her number instead to tell her, but she wasn't carrying her phone.

Today she is the most prominent symbol of my ambition and creative vision. But she wasn't an easy character to mould. Those days, I was dreaming big. Both time and resources were scarce. I demanded her undivided attention at all times. Manasi lived for the little things. She could endlessly spend idle hours watching the sunset. When a bud or fruit blossomed on the plants she nurtured, her joy knew no bounds. She could smile at a stranger and laugh without a reason.

As time passed, Manasi slowly learnt to give up that carefree living.

Be it food, hygiene, home décor, punctuality or rehearsals; even weights and sizes are monitored at my house. Her life had undergone a sea change even before she realized it. Her hands were once expert at processing milk and cottage cheese with coconuts and dry fruits, tossing out elaborate traditional Bengali sweets. Today the same hands concentrate on oats, idli and other such health foods that prevent unhealthy cholesterol.

I smile to myself, as I finish off the last sip of wine. If such elements have learnt to give up their meandering philosophies and fall in line with me, then so would Vatsala. I just hope that she knows what she is getting into.

Next morning, I drive off to New York University for an interaction with the students of Visual Culture and Cultural Studies. I am scheduled to deliver a speech on Bharatanatyam as an ancient, yogic culture for practising spiritualism. I ask for their thoughts on these distinct art forms and how their extinction can be prevented. The students ask a variety of questions too. Their doubts hover between the Bharatanatyam make-up and costumes which seem exotic and unusual in the context of the American culture, the themes and music, the postures and their specific spiritual meanings, and why a 'local art' like Bharatanatyam would always face the threat because of its dependence on Indian religious mythology which people from other religions or communities may not be accustomed to.

My jaw tightens at this last statement. It is true, and that's the purpose I believe I am born to serve. Bharatanatyam, in its purest element, can never liberate itself from its mythological roots. I don't believe in mixing two or more dance forms. I believe in restoring the true spirit and grammar of the art, and expressing emotions within pre-defined confines. Creative liberty lies in putting together an unthinkable act without trespassing the rules. Fusion is an easy means of giving pleasure, but it lacks the spiritual essence of pure art.

I explain my logic to the students. 'Fusion or mixed dance is like junk food. It serves its audience by holding their attention but harms their system and deprives them of the organic pleasure which they have actually come for. Like all junk foods, it has its side effects; they take the art away from its orthodox roots. New learners gain diluted knowledge which doesn't take them anywhere.'

After the lecture, I invite them to come and join my mission at the New York chapter of Kala Mandir. Soon after, the students and teachers bid me a warm farewell.

After attending some meetings with the DCA and representatives of the United Nations, I come back to the room at around eight in the evening. After the jet lag followed by a sleepless night and the rigour of an active day, my body aches as if I have fought a hundred thousand monsters. It refuses to move any further. The soft bed invites me to rest my overused bones under the warmth of the quilt. Without much delay, I drop off to sleep.

I wake up fresh, after a blissful eight-hour sleep. With my usual rituals of yoga, meditation and chants, I start yet another day abuzz with pre-scheduled activities. I step out of my room for breakfast. As I lock the room and turn, something hammers inside my heart.

I freeze.

Vatsala is sitting on a bench outside, on the balcony. Her head is rested on the railing. With one hand, she covers her eyes to block sunlight. She has put her legs up on the bench and covered her body with a shawl.

Did she knock on the door last night? Was I sleeping so deeply that I didn't even hear her approaching? I can't help but feel horribly guilty at the sight.

For a brief second, I am reminded of those mornings at our shabby orphanage, where the sun didn't penetrate till noon. And then the days when I sat on ill-placed benches outside the houses or offices of potential sponsors who could help me stage that first show. When auditoriums refused to give enough slots and stopped taking my calls, I would stand endlessly outside their offices or follow them wherever they went, to strike a deal at an opportune moment.

Has she been sitting here since 3 a.m., I wonder. It gets quite cold here at that hour. Slowly, and somewhat stealthily, I walk up to her.

15

Back to the Origin

MANASI
Mumbai, 2015

I have been studying the scriptures voraciously to build up a theme. I have only fourteen days to come up with a story. Most of my time goes in flipping through the pages of Indian mythological books, browsing over the internet and having long meetings with the senior members of Kala Mandir. All of them have been at my house for almost twenty-four hours now without a break. We study and brainstorm ideas that can be compiled into a conceivable theme.

It was Ali who suggested the first part of the plot.

'Akka, Krishna claims in the Gita that he is time. Time, which destroys and perishes and renews. Time, that is destiny, which can be controlled or altered by none. Why not explore the Krishna connection of Kali Ma in the beginning? Could Kali, who is the Goddess of destruction, be an extension of Krishna, the perennial lover who sways the world with his flute? The conflict here can be interesting.'

The team begins to actively research this.

Along with preparing the story board, we simultaneously also have to decide the formats of the dance. In sync with the event's theme, there has to be an interpretation of some classical piece of work, without violating the grammar of the art. Kala Mandir never does an amalgamation of different styles. However, certain themes are better interpreted when performers are less rigid about the style and plan movements intelligently to explore the space provided for a better presentation. But Shekhar wouldn't approve of mixed genres. I don't intend to create something ideologically different, but I certainly want my choreography to possess a distinct edge of my own, without meddling with the uniqueness and class of Kala Mandir. That would be my gift to Shekhar and Kala Mandir.

But I am not Shekhar. I can't multitask, dividing myself to execute ten different roles with equal ease. I have decided to divide the work between deserving members of Kala Mandir. Once individual components fall into place, we can together combine our expertise and collaborate to host the show. I haven't spelt this out to Shekhar, but I have already made a list of activities that can be outsourced and have written down which member of Kala Mandir would be the best choice to take over those sections forward independently.

In many mythological studies, the Krishna avatar of Vishnu is identified with Kali. In one of the Tantrik mystic traditions of Bengal, Goddess Kali, often addressed as Tara, is identified with Krishna's female form. Both share the same dark complexion, and their companions—Shiva in the case of Kali, and Radha in the case of Krishna are extremely fair, making their contrast, and hence the difference in purpose, even more prominent.*

As I immerse myself into researching the Kali–Krishna connection, I am drawn to some heavenly characters who, in deeds and destiny, philosophically merge into one. Within my mind, I can effectively feel that I am not too far away from the story I want to create and interpret, just that I need more substance that can add authenticity to the tale. I bring my papers closer, my head supported with pillows. Sleep is nowhere close.

My existence seems limited to the illuminated portions of the pages I hold.

In Vedic literature, the destructive and misery-laden nature of Time is represented by Goddess Kali, who inflicts various kinds of suffering on the inhabitants of this Universe. Kaal, or Time, in turn, controls Kali.**

Every religion preaches that the soul merges with the Divine at the end of life. The Bhagavad Gita explains that Lord Krishna desires celestial beings to surrender unconditionally to Him. Kali, thus, becomes his agent provocateur; she brings in sufferings as a result of materialistic ambitions and possessions, and paves the path to reach Krishna for ultimate salvation.

I pour almost a full bottle of water down my throat. Creating fictional content with reference to the scriptures have chances of backfiring. My brain wanders restlessly over multiple options which the act can use as a starting premise. For a while, I lift my eyes from the pages and move towards the window for some fresh air. In the pitch dark of amavasya outside, the sea is far from visible. It is hot and humid, and nature stands still. Not even

---

*http://devdutt.com/articles/from-kali-to-krishna-a-love-song.html
**http://devdutt.com/articles/from-kali-to-krishna-a-love-song.html

a leaf moves; there is no boat rowing on the sea, nor any sign of breeze and the path in front of the main gate looks desolate. Only a soft street light that trembles incessantly to signal the inevitable end of its service suggests that this silence too has life. The huge clock in the hall downstairs has just struck one.

My mind wanders, trying to touch upon something vast which is very much within my grasp; yet the moment I feel it enter my conscious understanding, it slips away!

Many versions of the Mahabharata contemplate upon the unique relationship between Krishna and Draupadi. Draupadi is also called Krishnaa, 'the dark one', because of her complexion. They both have a fondness for Arjuna. Born of her father's fire sacrifice, Draupadi was destined to bring upon destruction and become the cause of the biggest war in Indian mythological history. Research strongly considers Draupadi to be an incarnation of Kali, as she brought sufferings to many.

Wait! Draupadi had entered the Pandava clan as a new bride. The newly-wed bride is said to be the embodiment of Lakshmi,* and is considered to usher in prosperity into her matrimonial home. After the game of dice, when Pandavas were defeated and Dushshasana had disrobed Draupadi, did he then unknowingly invoke Kali? Draupadi's karmic connections with Kali may have been manifested in the Kaurava court, where their physical appearance too matched almost literally, and the Kuru prince never realized that his wrong-doing was calling for unimaginable destruction as he had unintendedly kindled the naked Goddess in the royal lady!

---

*Lakshmi: Vishnu's wife, Shiva and Parvati's daughter; goddess of prosperity and wealth

I sit up and start writing my own tale, interpreting philosophy and mythology in my own way. The story starts with Krishna narrating his journey through paradise, earth, and back to paradise, introducing the most unlikely companion who contrasts his beauty with her violence, his love with her fury, and his protection with her destruction. The black goddess, Kali!

Krishna's Monologue

Goddess Kali is the consort of Lord Shiva, also referred to as Shakti, meaning energy. Lord Shiva is the silent aspect of the Transcendental Reality, and Mother Kali is the dynamic aspect of the Transcendental Reality. When Kali is performing her role, reality is moving. When Shiva is performing, reality is silent. Shiva never spoke a single word until Shakti came into his life as Parvati. Parvati assumed different roles to fulfil Shiva's expectations from his wife. Shiva and Parvati are said to be the most ideal match. As Annapoorna, the goddess of food, she fed him. As Kamakhya, the goddess of pleasure, she indulged with him in exploring physical ecstasy. As Gauri, demure and delicate, she allowed Shiva to dominate, though she is beyond domination. As Durga, she protected. As Kali, undressed with hair unbound, undeterred to be herself, unafraid of being judged and mocked, she taught him to face the truth. Lalita, the beautiful, is also Bhairavi, the fearsome. Mangala, the auspicious, is also Chandika, the violent. By opening herself in totality for her Lord, Shakti allowed her true, complete self to be perceived by Shiva, thus assuming the role of a mirror which in turn helped Shiva to discover himself.*

Shiva asked Parvati to fulfil his last desire. He said, 'As Shyama, the dark Goddess, who is also Kali and Shakti, you have taught me love. You have danced atop me, forced me to open my eyes, turn from shava (corpse) to Shiva. Grant me the chance to do the same to you. I wish to love you as a woman, and want you to receive love like a man.' Thus, Shiva descended on earth as the fair Radha, whose prayers and longing would summon Shakti as her lover, and she would manifest in the world as the dark one, Krishna.**

Krishna and Kali, thus are one and the same!

Krishna, whom mortals call Vishnu and Narayan, and many other names, rests within the supreme soul. He is the super ego, the division between Dharma and Adharma, the politics behind half-truths that lead the path to righteous virtues, and also the futile innocence that submits itself to self-destructive pride.

Radha taught Krishna the meaning of love as Shakti had once taught Shiva. Just as Shakti transformed Shiva into Nataraj, Radha made Krishna take up the flute. Radha was demanding, as Parvati once had been. She sat on Krishna as Kali stood on Shiva. The two thus merged in roles and thoughts. There was just one difference. Parvati had turned the wandering Shiva into a rooted

---

*http://devdutt.com/articles/from-kali-to-krishna-a-love-song.html
**http://devdutt.com/articles/from-kali-to-krishna-a-love-song.html

hermit, Shankara. Radha did the very opposite. She remained a flower stuck to the branch of a tree while Krishna became the bee that moves on after enriching himself with the nectar. So, once fulfilled, Krishna left Radha's Madhuban for Mathura. Parvati had revealed love through shringara (romance), as only Krishna can. Radha revealed love through vairagya (renunciation), like only Shiva can.*

I, Krishna, the Supreme Being, am attached to Kali like the umbilical cord that connects the child to his mother. Without one, the other is incomplete, purposeless, incompetent. Kali symbolizes my language of Maya—the power of transition, transformation and illusion, and is also divinely responsible for renewing and rejuvenating the rugged and the rusted. Kali's fulfilment, however, rests in her unison with Shiva and balancing her diversion with Lakshmi, Durga and Parvati, who are extensions of her own self.

Here's inviting the world to experience the magnificence of this fierce beauty, who resides within one and all as much as I do, in her divine manifestation of Shakti—the power and Kala—the eternal time.

∽

When the sun brightens the eastern sky and waves lash the shore, I no longer have the strength to welcome them from

---

*http://devdutt.com/articles/from-kali-to-krishna-a-love-song.html

my favourite bedside window. On the table, in front of an open laptop, I lie down to rest my tired brain after the rigour of reading and writing all through the night.

My journey of self-exploration has just begun.

16

A Fresh Dawn

VATSALA PANDIT
Manhattan, 2015

I am sad and disappointed and I make no attempts to hide it.

'I had a crazy day at work, then went for my rehearsals and still made it here at 2.45 a.m. because you wanted me to. What a warm way to declare that you don't care a damn whether people looking up to you live or die!'

Shekhar doesn't look remorseful. In a very clumsy, dismissive way he extends an apology and offers to be back at a more humane time, around seven in the evening.

But I have come with other plans.

'No.' My voice still echoes my frustrations. 'Tonight, you have to be present at my show. Treat this as my CV, as my formal introduction to you as a follower of art.' He declines the invitation without wasting a moment, but I persist, and finally persuade him to attend. 'I will send a vehicle that will come to pick you up in the evening,' I mention before leaving.

A few hours later, I ensure he is being escorted in a car I sent, fearing that he might change his mind on the way. The car stops at The New School Auditorium at Chelsea. Shekhar is received warmly by the authorities and school organizers. Little enthusiasts offer him bouquets and cards, as he is ushered towards the VIP seat in front.

We have a ballet performance scheduled here. The next few hours are a roller coaster ride for the dancers, transporting the audience to a different world where we perform heavenly aerobics with the poetic movement of our bodies. Ballet requires inhuman balance and control over pelvic and abdominal muscles to design a story themed with classical perfection.

I am at the pinnacle of expertise here, with the fundamental techniques of my craft moulded to enhance the art rather than merely servicing the viewers. This evening is important, as seated gracefully amidst the audience is the ice-hearted.

The next few hours must change something for both of us!

We are playing the story of The Lady of Shallot, borrowing the theme from Lord Alfred Tennyson's celebrated creation. I play the Lady of Shallot, dressed in white. From a raised platform, I speak to myself through the imaginary mirror in front.

Another girl plays the mirror image, speaking back to me, absorbing and reflecting the lady's frustrations, sadness, longings, aspirations, cheerfulness and fears. We dance like twins mirroring each other, just like Shekhar's wife had done for 'Manipur Stotram'. I had carefully planned the choreographic resemblance to remind Shekhar where I was coming from. The steps pleasure as does an act of theft through the vigil of a stern guard. But that's me. If I am not allowed to take what I deserve, I steal it in style.

The Lady of Shallot is destined to weave a colourful magic

web and look at the world only through her mirror, failing which a curse would fall upon her. Dancers dressed in black play mysterious voices to warn her of the unavoidable misfortune if she would choose to violate her destiny.

One day a knight comes riding through the fields and his jewels reflect on the Lady's mirror. For a split second, she forgets about her curse and looks out. The sound of the mirror cracking into pieces and strong winds that blow her web away echo across the auditorium. She prepares herself for the last time to go out to the world and sail through the Camelot singing her divine song as she falls to her death.

Next evening when I meet the Dancer, he seems quite a different person.

I smile to myself, raising a flag of victory within my heart. Not that his domination has come down by an atom, but he looks more accommodative towards me. At least he receives me nicely and congratulates me on the performance. This is enough to get me flying high with butterflies in the stomach. However, I keep my excitement in wraps, scared that the whimsical patriarch will return to his cocoon of tough silence if I express too much. For the first time in life I accept compliments with a shy smile instead of demanding beer parties.

This is just the start, I promise myself. I shall crack him a million times in the days to come.

I am guided inside to the huge open portico in the backyard which is comparatively vacant and uninhabited. A soft light makes things visible for passers-by, while a mild breeze touches more than the skin. Unsure of what is in store, my heart leaps once again at the romantic possibilities of such an ambience.

We walk separately but our shadows touch each other more than once. They aren't as unfriendly as we are. I smile as they come together and drift apart, unplanned, playfully nudging each other as we move. He stops a few steps ahead. I halt too, and turn away from him, adjusting myself within the frame of his shadow as intimately as I can. My thin build is now engulfed within his large, shapely silhouette. I chuckle.

He calls out from behind.

I let myself fall backwards. My head hits softly against his spinal cord, stopping me from falling any further. He turns and encircles my neck with his arm, his mouth just near my ears. I hear him breathe. For once, he looks at me with the longing of a lifetime. I close my eyes. I lean on Shekhar's broad chest, place my hands encircling his neck bringing myself very close to his lips. He smells divine. I expect his hands to come upwards through the small of my back.

When that doesn't happen, I look around and the daydream shatters.

I try to guess what must be occupying his fantasies at this hour. The face is dark, quite disconnected from my adventures. He is busy removing his shoes. I mutter a curse and start undoing mine hastily to keep pace with him. From the corner of my eye, I find him staring at my feet. He seems uncharacteristically lost in a tattoo on my ankle I got done a few months ago. I open my mouth to explain what the symbol means, but stop as obscure, distant eyes render me speechless.

With what the hunk speaks next, the romance in my heart breathes its last.

17

The Unexpected Beginning

RAJ SHEKHAR SUBRAMANIAN
Manhattan, 2015

The ballet was a revelation of sorts. I am genuinely touched by the skills of the troupe. The death scene of the Lady of Shallot especially, had been captured with surreal metaphors where artistes in grey and blue harmonized their movements to create waves symbolizing underwater radiance and the melancholy of death, both at the same time. Vatsala put up an act where she flew all across the stage balancing herself on the tip of one foot, with infrequent support of the other leg which was otherwise raised backwards. For a moment, I focussed on her feet trying to decipher whether she was wearing wheels. She wasn't.

The experience of watching the splendour of another culture ushers in an artistic resurrection. The world knows that it isn't so easy to impress me to this extent.

I can't ignore, insult or underestimate this woman any longer. A connection is born. A performer recognizes another's creative instincts. Her footwork would be worth dying for in my Bharatanatyam. I will build her up, step by step, just like

I had created many others in my troupe.

Keeping up with the wandering means of this girl though, is a test of patience. I am reminded of that on the very next day when she appears at my portico.

Lost somewhere in her own dreams, she seems to have entered my guest house purposeless. Her delight to be standing here is never-ending. She takes time to get the hint as I remove my shoes, then hurriedly gets on to the job. In fact, she doesn't remove her sneakers; she kicks them off her feet as if they were a burden. Her shoes and socks fall at a distance, showing their owner's negligence. I sigh sadly. Affluence hasn't allowed her to value things she owns quite easily. In my early twenties, I was struggling hard to make ends meet. Expensive shoes like the ones she has so casually discarded could not be a part of my wardrobe during my youth. Even later, after opulence knocked, my personal habits have always adhered to my values. Manasi has stood by me like a rock, supporting those choices always.

On Vatsala's left leg, just above the ankle, there is a tattoo. Something written in Arabic, I guess. Illegible, but artistic, and certainly beyond my understanding, the inscribed letters shine bright on her fair skin. It looks bohemian and sinful, unlike another pair of feet with the soft shrill sound of mysterious anklets, following everywhere that Manasi goes. That music, which has Manasi's rhythm embedded within its informal beats, stays in my subconscious like a gentle lullaby even when she is not around.

Her anklets had rung out loud with gusto when I had started teaching her Bharatanatyam for the first time in that small secluded room in Bangalore. Nervously, she had tried to remove them to put an end to the distracting jingle. I advised her to make peace with the indiscipline of those little silver bells.

I turn my concentration back on to the mini audio player I am carrying.

'You told me that you have picked up some of our Bharatanatyam compositions and can replace any of my dancers with remarkable ease. Name a composition that you are comfortable with and I will play the music. I need to see where you stand.'

Vatsala seems rudely transported back from her fantasies. She takes a while to absorb the instruction and prepares herself to start in haste. Almost immediately she stands dumb struck as I shout, 'Stop.' The player goes dead.

'Never start before you have bowed to the earth.'

The girl looks puzzled. Of course, it isn't her fault if she doesn't know this. Manasi didn't know either, in her first session with me after our marriage.

Calmly I explain it to Vatsala, perhaps repeating the same words that I used some seventeen years ago.

'You trouble Mother Earth with your feet when you dance, but the mother in return gives you base and balance. Before every performance, however small or insignificant, never forget that you owe your gratitude to the mother. So please pull your hands up, stretch them backwards and bring them straight down to touch the ground. Don't bend your knees. And then pull yourself back to your position and start.'

For the next three hours, I play the music from various compositions. I make a mental note of all her strengths and flaws. The girl has picked up our compositions with due diligence. In my mind, I credit her for the sincerity.

We pick up coffee from the cafeteria at the end of the session. Vatsala sits on the stairs instead of walking up to the tables, taking me by surprise once again. I stand for a while as she looks up expecting me to do the same.

'It's nice from here,' she smiles, 'You can see everyone and even the shrubs and roses that cover the fence.'

I rest myself on a step above her, leaning across the wall and sipping my coffee. Vividly I recall how Manasi had fallen on me after her first day of training, all the weight of her body and mind descending on my chest.

Some moments pass in silence. Though I am not looking at her, I can see Vatsala thinking of possible ways to initiate a conversation. I disappoint her again.

'A lot of your movements were taking you back to ballet, Vatsala. I could see that you have tried to copy our expressions with meticulous perseverance. But, many times the ballet dancer in you took over your subconscious and your body responded. Bharatanatyam is all about grammar and technique; you can't be meddling with that.'

I pause for a while and sip the coffee. 'Bring your sensuousness in Abhinaya or Naatya of Bharatanatyam.'

Vatsala's eyes light up as I say this; I pretend to not notice.

'I can predict that this will be one of your future strengths while performing. I know it won't be easy for you, given that you carry the baggage of a beautiful art and you are an expert at it. I'm there to guide you, but you'll have to be mentally prepared for some gruelling days ahead. During my sessions, don't treat yourself as an accomplished ballet dancer. Remember, and feel that you are a novice.'

'You found it sensuous yesterday?' Is all that she has to ask? The girl doesn't let go of a single chance to flirt. I glance at her and look away.

'Why did you want me to go for your ballet performance?' I steer the conversation on a different path making peace with the fact that the girl won't change her means overnight just because I don't approve of them.

'I wanted you to respect me!' She pauses and looks away, talking almost to herself. 'I do have my talents, you know. Fine, I have come to you like a smitten fan, but does that really give you the right to treat me like dirt?'

A very dark allegation. I choose my words wisely. 'I do respect everyone. But if I were to meet everyone who comes to my doorstep, I won't have time for Bharatanatyam. I don't worship anyone or anything more than my art. That is why admirers come to me. Vatsala, I would advise you to focus your passion on Bharatanatyam rather than on me.'

I get up and walk off. Not only has my patience been drained for the day but I also battle the thrust of an unexpected demand.

∽

'I wanted you to respect me!'

This is a strange wish I have never heard before.

The last time I judged someone's amateur performance as a professional Bharatanatyam artiste was when I had found Manasi dancing to the dhaak in Kolkata. Her innocence, her smiles, her large eyes, all come flooding back to me.

Not sure why these memories suffocate me tonight. Maybe because then and now, the situation is almost the same. Then I was looking forward to set up my dance academy and pursue my dreams as a dancer. Today, I am again on a similar journey, rebuilding the academy in a different country, unsure of whether I will be accepted or dumped. It is just that now, Manasi has been replaced by Vatsala.

While teaching Manasi, I had the comfort of her trust. With Vatsala, I have to constantly confront her demands. The contrast is too strong to overlook. Weirdly though, both women in their individual capacities, distinctly distinguished from each other, have pronounced my dream as theirs.

As I enter the elevator with slow steps, I stop, shocked. I am deeply embarrassed, realizing that I have been comparing Manasi with Vatsala! Irritated beyond soothing, I pull my hair backwards between my fingers, attempting to brush off any irrelevant thoughts.

Vatsala's last few words and my immediate response to that has made me face some fundamental questions.

'I do respect everyone,' I had told her.

Really? Do I?

The woman who has been serving me with her body and soul, have I respected her? Have I respected her enough? Have I ever bothered to understand the talents she may have brought with her as an individual, which were not necessarily captured in the instructions I always burdened her with?

In my room, I pace up and down with unfamiliar restlessness. I want to reach out to Manasi right now. I want to find out if there's another woman hidden somewhere inside my wife.

Within the upper shell of unconditional love, is there another face which is tired of me?

What would she look like as an independent woman, who is not brutally carved as per the expectations of her husband?

18

The Biography

BRIAN HERRETT
Manhattan, 2016

Freshly brewed coffee reminds me of some breezy dates.

The same beverage helps Shekhar to sit resignedly in the balcony at Manhattan and introspect. Just a day after the inaugural show, those muscles must be hurting. Shekhar obviously wouldn't confess. But his energy is abnormally low. He needs to sleep, but he won't tell me that either. He wants to talk.

Manasi's voice floats in from somewhere; Shekhar lifts his eyes to look for her. She isn't visible. Carefully I toss over a question, a rather blunt one, praying in my heart that Shekhar doesn't take offence. He doesn't.

'Shekhar, given another chance, would you be less harsh on Vatsala? She is an artiste too. Shouldn't you have handled her with some affection?'

The Master breathes deep till the air touches his lungs.

'Brian,' He says. 'When you grow up experiencing scarcity at different levels, you either become a recluse who doesn't care what goes and what remains, or you become a miser, protecting and saving whatever you have accumulated. I am the latter.' He laughs. 'My principles, my pride, Manasi—these are my accumulations—the ones that I am too protective and miserly about!'

'You are conservative.' I laugh too. 'But Shekhar, you didn't do that just because you already had a wife. There is more to it.'

Shekhar smiles again, nodding at the way I probe. 'Yes, there is. All my life I have chased after some kind of perfection. My understanding of perfection may have been flawed by some standards, but it worked for me. Vatsala was a threat to my definition of correctness. This certainly was a lot about Manasi, but not really because of that cliché dilemma between wife and the other woman. Vatsala was never the *other woman* in my world; she was my student. Only my student. But Vatsala didn't think so. She pushed it very hard. And I couldn't bring her out of it.'

Shekhar pauses, breathing a little too fast. I hand him a glass of water. He ignores it.

'Manasi made me and everyone else believe that I am perfect. A perfect husband, a perfect dancer, a perfect teacher, a perfect human being. She has always been that steady emotional cushion I needed so much to march ahead. Vatsala did just the opposite. Not only had she challenged my world of perfection, but she also brought me to face how incomplete my giving was to Manasi. My heart wanted to cast her off; my brain knew she was right; and my system revolted because of the sheer realization that I could not undo all those delicate moments I messed up while pursuing a hollow excellence.'

Unmindfully his eyes hover somewhere far away, preparing to articulate a difficult confession.

'For years Manasi allowed me to feel that she is nothing without me. I almost grew up on that pride. Vatsala proved right in the beginning, that had she not intervened, we wouldn't have been here fulfilling a dream in Manhattan. She made me look back and acknowledge my dependence on Manasi! Truth hurts at times, my friend. She felt like a disaster in the life I had constructed so carefully…with and for myself.'

He looks at me. 'You said I am conservative? True, that. And heartless, too, in many ways.'

Shekhar picks up the glass of water and gulps it down to quench a thirst that has persisted for long. My recorder records that sound too. Perhaps he is miserably trying to force down something that chokes his throat and his heart.

19

The Restructuring

MANASI
Mumbai, 2015

Every hour of my days is spent with the team now. All classes are pushed to the evenings. In the mornings, everyone meets with a fresh brain and renewed energy to plan out the upcoming event. All members of the core team research and choreograph together, share their ideas and discuss how best to take the composition forward. I take down rigorous notes and study the progress of the day at night. It feels, at times, like a never-ending picnic. Many times, the team stays back at night because it gets too late and their day starts early. They talk about the show, make fun of each other and share from each other's plates on the dinner table. This has never happened before. There is always a certain degree of formality when Shekhar is around.

It is a Saturday afternoon. All members of Kala Mandir have gathered in the hall. I call out to everyone, 'Since Shekhar is not there all of us have to collectively build up what he does singlehandedly. Let us grow out of his safe shelter and bring our personal learning and expertise to the table. We just have to sail through this to support Shekhar at this hour.'

Everyone exchanges glances, unsure of what is coming up.

I read out from a notepad, 'Following are the duties I have allotted; tell me if you all are fine with this arrangement.'

I look around for a confirmation, then read on, 'Ali and Varanya will be in charge of research and choreography along with me.' Both of them nod their heads in agreement.

'Sulochana, your background into Hindustani classical and Carnatic music must help us create some fresh tracks we need at this hour. You and Emraan will be looking after the music.'

Sulochana and Emraan raise their hands for a high-five.

'Natarajan would do up the lights; ask Tashi to join in; I'll have a word with her. Costumes and the looks of each dancer would be designed by Siddharth and Sunanda.' I look at Sunanda. 'Sandy, you pair up with Sid, but don't remain so sweet always; else he will dominate you.' Sandy smiles quietly, and I go back to the papers in hand.

I turn to Dhriti.

'Dhriti, your poetic fantasies need to translate into some dreamy ideas to help us plan the stage.' I look to her left. 'Arjun will coordinate with you to analyse the investment and returns. Our designs must align with the budget.'

Arjun sits up suddenly, shocked. I control my laughter. 'Akka!' he protests, but I interrupt before he says anything further. 'This is not the time when we can afford to keep up with your legendary ego fights, Arjun. Two talented resources of Kala Mandir can't stay apart just because they are strong-headed and short-tempered.' I put the papers aside and bend towards them. 'Why should you guys remain so adamant about your differences when together you can create wonders?'

Arjun can't contain himself any further. 'Akka, please!' he says. 'This Bangalan's* tastes are a few feet above the ground. She is the goddess of extravagance; her ideas are impractical. I hate misusing or wasting money. How can I work with her?'

Dhriti retorts angrily, 'This Maru** loves to act difficult. He says that he believes in retaining and sustaining, but actually he is a miser. Accept it, loser!'

I stop them from bickering any further. 'That's not correct. The truth is, Dhriti's poetic detachment contrasts with Arjun's strong presence in each moment of his life. It's just as simple or as complicated as you want it to be,' I say firmly and turn to Dhriti. 'Arjun is blessed with an excellent memory. He never misses out on any instruction. And he is fast. So, when Dhriti shares an idea, which we all know will be soaked in poetic grace, Arjun will measure its practical possibilities and point out the pros and cons in every minute detail. And together, you both design the stage. Is that a problem?' My voice sounds uncharacteristically sharp. 'If it is, then I'll tell Shekhar that his team is too engrossed in their immature personal battles, so he must forget about this New York idea and come back to Mumbai.' I throw the notepad away.

Stunned at this rare voicing of my displeasure, Arjun quickly gets up to pick up the notepad and hands it back to me. He and Dhriti nod their heads, unhappy, but left with no other choice. They make faces at each other.

---

*Bangalan: slang for someone from Bengal
**Maru: slang for Marwari, hailing from the business community of Rajasthan

I look at Natarajan. 'Fine, then. Natarajan, where's Tashi? Would you please ask her to see me sometime?'

Natarajan agrees to bring his Manipuri wife, Tashi, to see me in the evening. I leave the room. As I walk through the corridor, Sid comes running from behind and walks with me.

'Akka, you really mean Sandy and I can do up the looks and costumes all by ourselves?' he asks, sounding excited.

I smile. 'You are the one interning with some fashion designer. Who else can I trust with this job?'

Sid looks worried. 'But what if Anna doesn't like my work?'

'You go ahead and do your best; the responsibility is mine.'

Sid hugs me and runs back to the hall. I smile at his enthusiasm. At least one person in the team is approaching the job head on. Thanks to the sincere parallel pursuit of designing, Sid exactly knows what features to accentuate and which to play down, so that the character portrayed by the performer becomes visually attractive. I know he won't disappoint.

In the next few days, I find Sandy, though elder than him by quite some years, assuming the role of his trusted executor. Calm and quiet herself, she has become strangely protective about the notoriously innocent Sid. Their tastes and attitudes towards life are vastly different, but she perfectly understands what Sid means by 'rain-washed yellow' or 'sun-burnt orange'. I have a feeling that she will work out his vision to perfection. Their equation amuses me no end.

Sunanda Bhardwaj. This Himachali Brahmin came to us with orthodox religious sentiments. It had taken her quite some time to let go of her family-run rigidity to embrace the Kala Mandir culture. Sunanda is always the first one from Kala Mandir to join Shekhar in his morning prayers. She can recite his chants even in her sleep. Usually she joins him in the temple even before I do. Compared to Sid's vibrancy, she is shy and soft-spoken. Sid makes fun of her; Sandy smiles quietly, but never returns personal attacks in protest.

As the Sid-Sandy duo jumps into work, I simultaneously start working further on my script.

It is very early in the morning when Sulochana, Emraan and I, along with some others, sit in Shekhar's study working on 'Krishna's Monologue'. The mridang player, Suraj, joins us. I watch them discuss the plans and grow increasingly restless.

Sulochana says, 'A lot of sound effects will have to be included to add to the ambience. I think Anna would like the lashing sound of waves and conch shells in abundance to mark Krishna's entry.'

Emraan stops her. 'Look guys, as per Akka's script...'

I interrupt. 'It's "our" script, Emraan, not my script.'

Emraan looks confused, but soon he gets the point. 'Yes, as per our script, after the monologue Krishna would stand still, giving space to a group of eight dancers to perform the Mangalam. The Mangalam would invoke Goddess Kali, and Krishna would disappear. Anna knows the flow till here.'

He consults some papers in his hands. 'Then Akka would take the stage amidst the music of the flute, to symbolize Kali's soulful connection to Krishna. We have prepared a musical theme for this using violin, flute, mridang, manjira, veena and kanjira.' He looks at me and stops abruptly. 'Can we record it and send across to Anna?'

Sulochana stops him. 'Hey, wait. What if Anna rejects this?

The theme uses flute prominently in the beginning and later manjira and kanjira gain precedence to accompany the visually strong emotions of Kali. Let's try to embellish it with stotras* and chants picked up selectively from Krishna Purana, Shiva Chalisa, Durga Chalisa and Kalika Purana. Only after that we can email it to Anna.' She looks at Emraan, and then at me.

Everyone else nods in agreement.

'The raga malika** is based on chants and instrumental music, composed predominantly on Raga Bhairav. Last year Anna had done the "Krishna Leela" on Raga Bhairav, remember? Sulochana and I are spending lots of time in the music room with the singers and players to get the beats, rhythms and chants carved into our minds,' Emraan informs the group.

He picks up the mridang and starts playing the instrument himself with his usual zest.

'Stop, guys!' I say, my impatience quite visible.

Everyone is surprised. Emraan stops playing and looks up.

I feel hopeless. 'You are thinking about Shekhar more than the pros and cons of a new idea. Stop holding back just because you need Shekhar's approval. Please. Make yourselves happy with your contributions. Take charge of your individual selves and listen to your unique creative capacities. Why don't you understand? Visualize and be prepared to experience the success of your own concepts that you believe, can create wonders. It is important for you all, and for Shekhar as well.'

I try to calm down a little. 'I know it is difficult to pull

---

*Stotras: Sanskrit verses
**Raga malika: a medley with various compositions of Hindustani classical music

ourselves out of the lingering habit of staying awestruck with Shekhar; this sudden freedom to follow our hearts and bring it back to the table as creative input might sound like an unrealistic goal. But I'm afraid we will have to force a change almost overnight!'

I look at everyone. Their faces are blank. They stare at me as though I were speaking Hebrew.

'Guys, prepare yourselves to defend your themes even if I or Shekhar feel that they are not good enough. Discuss it with us. Allow us to learn something back from you.'

I know I have shocked them. Everyone looks baffled. But this had to happen. No point postponing the inevitable.

Ali is the most disturbed. In his mind, Shekhar is God. He makes no attempt to hide how disturbed he feels. 'Akka, you are actually asking too much from us. What are we trying to achieve by doing this? We can't ever put up a show even remotely equivalent to what Anna does alone, even when we work collectively.'

I let out a deep sigh. 'For you, obedience is the best form of love, Ali. For me, it is all about ensuring that Shekhar gets what he wants. I will work towards this, even if that comes at the cost of temporary disobedience,' I say softly. He looks up.

'Till now, I too have been just a follower of Shekhar. But now, the time demands all of us to grow, so that Shekhar feels confident about us. Only then Shekhar can grow as well. Our dependence is a shortcoming for him in the days to come; don't you realize?' My words spoken slowly, seem to be sinking in.

Ali stares at me for a while, then takes the back of my palms and rubs his eyes against them, confirming his support.

We are about to disperse, when Siddharth enters with Sunanda.

'Akka, I think the costumes of Krishna and Kali should be colour coordinated so that the visual connection between the two is retained. After much deliberation, Sandy and I have decided to go with dark violet rather than the more common blue. What do you think? Here's the look of both, complete with costumes and accessories,' he says and hands over a file. 'I am yet to work on Shiva.'

Both of them wait to hear me out.

I flip through the pages and smile in relief. I give them a thumbs-up. 'That's the spirit. Go for it, guys!'

20

The Inevitable Path

VATSALA PANDIT
Manhattan, 2015

I never imagined this training thing could be so thankless and unforgiving. The Dancer seems to be absolutely closed to the simple word called fun. He approaches life as if it is an endless list of tasks. I feel thrilled every time his attention hovers uncompromisingly on my face and body, churning out difficult artsy moments, but beyond Bharatanatyam he is distant and cold. It's weird that after a day's hard work someone can have the strength or will to give exhaustive dance lessons to a stranger, and nothing else!

Yes, I am a stranger to this man, in every sense of the word. I have tried all tricks but found it impossible to break the ice. Let alone a romantic signal, he doesn't even care to smile or acknowledge my presence within his scheme of things. Mechanically, he interacts with me just during the few hours when he helps me with those discipline-bound movements of the body. Otherwise he never obliges me with any affection. He doesn't waste a single word to know more about me or tell me about himself.

At times, his body is so close; his face, mouth and neck so reachable, I touch him pretending an accidental stretch of the hand. When he touches me back, his fingers helping me to posture mine right, the professional obligation doesn't adhere to any pretence.

And still, I consider myself special. How many students are fortunate enough to learn from Raj Shekhar Subramanian? How many people are allowed to touch him and be touched with those magnificent long fingers, though they mean nothing! Hardly anyone in the subcontinent has ever stood so close to his chest and experienced him sweat his muscles out while performing unusual techniques. The yoga with which I am made to begin the sessions do pleasant things to my body and mind. Every day I feel I have crossed an extra mile in some secret personal journey. I am brimming with a mysterious energy.

I wish there was a huge mirror somewhere close to the portico, where I could watch my slender body beside Shekhar's strong torso and observe how we look together. I want to match with his elegance as we practise. I dream of achieving resolute perfection in the art, so that my compatibility and chemistry with the Dancer become so prominent that he won't ignore me any longer.

And yet, every evening after the sessions I go back deprived.

This evening I leave office after a particularly hectic day, look at the watch and increase my pace. A colleague calls me from behind. I look back to find her running forward to walk with me.

'When will you reach the venue, Vat?'

I frown, as I keep walking briskly. 'What venue?'

The colleague looks shocked. Almost immediately I remember.

'Oh, Ray's party! I'm not coming, Jennice; got something important to do.'

Jennice can't believe what she hears. 'Something more important than Ray's birthday bash? Even last year you were dancing till four in the morning. What's wrong with you?'

I smile. 'Almost everything is wrong with me.' I sigh. 'I can't make it Jennice; you guys go, have fun, and sleep with him.' I wink.

Jennice winks back. 'So, are you sleeping with someone else?'

'I wish!' Sighing longer, once again, I walk ahead leaving Jennice behind, my steps unmindfully slow.

I have literally abandoned my active social life to learn Bharatanatyam in the evenings. What started as love for a foreign art has transformed into an unrelenting passion for the artiste as well. Or maybe it is the other way round; I am not sure. I want to be with him, where he is at his best. I want to stand with him on the stage. I want Shekhar to think of me every time he needs someone with him to invoke life into his artistic fantasies. I want to be indispensable to him.

His non-response causes my insides to burn.

I want to talk to him. I want him to take more interest in me; to value me. I wish that one evening he would walk with me till the Hudson or enjoy a concert with me at Times Square. Or simply, I wish he would tell me what's happening with his preparations for the New York chapter of Kala Mandir, who he is meeting, what's transpiring, and that he needs my assistance into all the areas in which I can contribute and create a difference. I stop and look at the sky.

Can't we just sit sometime talking endlessly about stuff? Is that too much to ask for?

I want to tell him about the aspirations I am chasing to build up a future of my choice, the adventure and excitement in challenging the mundane that inspires me like nothing else, the beauty in spontaneity and unpredictability that I have chased with all my being, and my love for everything that is forbidden!

Shekhar can't see that just like him, I too find myself in the beauty of the world. Only, my understanding of beauty is not so rigidly bound in just one form of art. My senses register a strange hunger to capture the charm of the living and non-living world, starting from the bedside mirror which reflects back a cheerful face early in the morning and ending in the night sky studded with the galaxies that I don't know much about, yet love staring at from my balcony, with a can of beer in hand.

I love Bharatanatyam because I want to be a part of that ravishing self-transformation. Learning the dance is also a typical way of challenging myself with something I almost knew nothing about some time back. Within a very few years, I have acquired a lot to rave about. There is a strange kick in testing the limits and subjecting oneself uncompromisingly to new adventures, only to emerge victorious at the end of the day. I refuse to believe, with an obstinate arrogance, that anything on earth is prohibited.

I didn't realize when I walked up the Brooklyn Bridge. Standing almost in the middle, I look back. At the end of the bridge, there is adulation waiting for me. People who love me, want me, are crazy about me, would do anything for me if I only drop a hint. I dominate over them, neglect them and make myself available at my whims and fancies. The other path leads to Shekhar, who hardly cares whether or not I exist. He wouldn't even realize if I don't go there this evening. Probably he would just find himself some other job, happy that his time is well-saved and channelized to some other cause.

Yet, something about that way tells me that my soul lies caged there. I can't run away even if I want to. Everything else would fade away with time; only what I build up there would remain. I wouldn't miss the party when I am at the portico, putting my frame through the postures of Bharatanatyam. But if I was at the party today, I would keep wondering what might have happened in Shekhar's backyard and my drink would remain unattended.

I walk faster, looking at my watch once again. I am almost running through the crowd, eager to reach a destination which certainly doesn't end at the guest house.

21

A Vast Terrace

MANASI
Mumbai, 2015

This evening, everyone has dispersed on account of their own engagements. I am glued to my computer to put together the rest of the act. It has been a tiring day. My concentration betrays me every other moment. My brain, heavy with an overload of information, begs for a break. I lean on the back of the chair and close my eyes.

For quite a while I haven't seen Shekhar. His phone calls are erratic as his schedule in New York often doesn't follow a strict timeline. Even if meetings end punctually, someone or the other stays back to talk more and settle things formally. Otherwise he has visitors. Important office holders of the state, organizers, embassy personnel, even novelists and sometimes filmmakers drain him of his time. Our conversations are becoming increasingly customary.

Downstairs Emraan and Suraj are playing the mridang. Beats reverberate all through the house like some holy unforeseen announcement. The music sounds like Shekhar. Dominating, royal, and in a strange way, lonely!

I open my eyes and look around. There is no visible difference between Shekhar being in the city and not being there. Even when he is in the house, he spends most of his time in the study. But in the vacant room, I can feel his absence. I get up from her chair to take a stroll around. Everyone and everything occupy their prescribed places. Yet everything feels so much out of place.

I walk into his study. There are no books to be picked up and kept back in place. In our bedroom, I open Shekhar's cupboard. The male odour engulfs me with a very familiar warmth.

Shekhar's being there at home or simply waiting for him to return gives my life its music. Things are very barren without him.

With all the years we spent together, now I can just feel his vibes.

Shekhar is too conscious of himself, his choices and his sophistication, even in bed! It's different however, when Shekhar draws in closer on early mornings. Half in sleep and half awakened to desire, he pulls me towards himself as lazy hands move softly over my body. Slowly we both wake up to the passion and surrender ourselves. On such mornings, Shekhar leaves his conscious mask behind.

I feel a sensation running down my spine. Could be the memory or the cool breeze. I clutch myself with both hands.

In Bangalore, soon after our wedding, all we could afford was a one-room kitchen flat with a small extended veranda. Shekhar invested whatever money we saved at the end of the month, so that the amount would give us sufficient returns upon maturity. Like other families in the same building, I never treated the balcony as a store room. I kept that part of the house as clean as the rest of it. We would sit there every morning with our tea, enjoying the breeze and chirping of the birds outside. On nights when Shekhar fell into a deep sleep at the end of a hard day, I quietly left the bed to stand on the balcony. The moon looked huge from there. I waited for Shekhar to turn sides, stretch a hand to touch me on the bed, realize that I am not there beside him and come out looking for me. Together we sat on the floor, I leaned to rest my head on his shoulders, shivering a little with the cool breeze, and listened to his plans about an ambitious future. The memories, the moments! They bring back a smile on my lips this desolate evening.

Today I own an entire terrace.

One end of the terrace faces the vast expanse of the Arabian Ocean, the other opens to some beautiful bungalows, apartments, gardens and parks built around the house. A considerable stretch of the Band Stand is visible from the terrace. I walk ahead towards the railing. Young couples hold hands and walk on the pavement near the sea. Some desperate ones sit too close to each other, engaging in activities that sanity doesn't permit in public. I move away.

This carefree, boundless romance lasts till people have nothing to lose. Between me and Shekhar, there has always been a distinct, uncompromised purpose that impairs any scope for romantic desperations, even behind closed doors. Our romance is more about trust and commitment; about belonging to each other with a faith that nothing else is more important to either than the joint dream we relentlessly pursue. And in chasing that dream, both Shekhar and I have grown together, though in vastly different ways. Shekhar has grown more cautious, caring and dominating with time. I have acquired the role of a loving wife who is more uncomplicated and finds her own joys in being and in letting others be.

The upcoming show is a test of whatever I have learnt from Shekhar.

While Shekhar is busy expanding Kala Mandir in another country, I am driven by the pursuit of a different kind of expansion within our existing formats. I want the minds of every member of Kala Mandir to explore beyond the boundaries of their comfort zones.

I will also prove to Shekhar that his first baby has grown up now and can take things upon itself independently. As much as the dancers of Kala Mandir have remained confined to Shekhar's plans and methodologies, Shekhar is equally confined to mentoring them on a microscopic level. My soul vows to liberate Shekhar from this confinement so that he can venture ahead without having to bother about any unfinished job that he is leaving behind.

As the last bit of light fades into darkness, the smell of camphor and incense sticks in the temple travels all across the house. I enter and pick up the conch shell to blow it long and smooth, just like I did all through my childhood.

22

The Uncanny Contrast

RAJ SHEKHAR SUBRAMANIAN
Manhattan, 2015

Spending time with this woman is a pleasure as much as it is a pain. She is an artiste who dances as if she'd perish if she didn't. As I reorganize her skills, I can see her gathering momentum with every passing day. She is determined to be flawless as much as I am stubborn to not accept anything less than that.

But I have to remain alert about her ways and means. She throws clues randomly to rip me off my diplomacy. My strict aloofness keeps her at bay. That doesn't stop her from playing with my patience and principles.

One day, she calls me in the morning. I don't answer her calls. Later she confronts me.

'What if something came up and I can't come in the evening, and I need to inform you of that?'

I respond without looking at her, 'Not my problem. Just be careful that I don't read your dedication as something superficial. For anything that needs to be conveyed urgently, there is something called an SMS.'

At the end of her sessions she tries to linger on with some excuse or the other. I ignore all her attempts.

One of these days during the regular routine, she looks at me with despair, expecting me to understand that her body is paining and she needs to call it a day. She is probably tired after a long day at office. Her eyes speak of severe discomfort. I remain inert to those signals. I want to know how far she is willing to stretch herself. Here, I am taking three times the stress, and at the age of 40! Every day, even after my mind and body are drained out of life, I make myself available to teach her. I show no mercy to her fatigue, which makes her livid.

'Repeat,' I instruct after we work on a fresh composition.

'Sadist,' I hear her murmur as she prepares to redo the composition. 'My ache is giving him entertainment.'

'Are you sure you want to say what you just said?' I ask coldly.

The floodgates open to pour out her agony. 'Can you tell me what makes you such a dark, self-obsessed individual? Can't you just let go of your inhibitions and stop treating me like an imposter? I am no less dedicated than you are. Just that I have a life, and you, on the other hand, practise saintly renunciation. Nothing or no one exists within a huge radius of your being. You are neither happy, nor sad. Neutrality is not life, you know? It's just as mechanical as breathing in and breathing out and nothing thereafter!' she utters angrily.

Accustomed to her ranting by now, I show no signs of remorse. 'Nothing comes easy in life. If you wish to win something then you have to pay a price for it. It requires sacrifice.'

Vatsala vigorously shakes her head.

'Sacrifice!' she repeats with disgust and gulps down water from her bottle. 'That is such a negative word!'

I frown. Vatsala forces a sarcastic smile while rubbing her right ankle with her hand. 'Sacrifice comes with a state of deprivation, sir. I never sacrifice anything. Prioritizing might be a more appropriate word.'

I turn pale.

Shocking the girl with an abrupt closure to the evening, I walk upstairs and close the door of my room, a dark realization growing inside my brain like the drone of a poisonous insect. Manasi has always kept my priorities ahead of her wishes. Never did I have the time or virtue to understand if she ever wanted something different. My life stands erect on the mountain of her sacrifices. It is probably too late for me to mend those.

Did she ever blame me for that? Did her body ache on tired nights, when I made her slog like a monster? Does she feel deprived? In our perfect journey, did I miss out on her personal priorities which, till date, I believed there were none?

I don't know!

Soft memories tease me like the touch of a feather. The partition of her hair that she stains with vermillion every morning; her smiles that light up my dreary days; her eyes wet with tears when I left her alone at the airport, yet an absorbing determination to hold them back so that I am not inconvenienced; those evenings when I would catch her watching the waves, standing alone at our bedside window. They tend to come back warning of something obscure arising from the horizon, the depth of which is beyond my competence to see or comprehend. They unsettle my reserve and meddle with my concentration.

God knows for how long I have been standing here, mulling over the days Manasi and I have spent together. This doesn't happen to me often. But I am oceans apart from her, stationed alone for days. On dark nights when I stretch my hand out only to find an empty bed, these memories are probably the only comfort I can offer myself. Who knows better than me, how terrible this loneliness is! These deserted nights scare me. I don't ever want to be left again in some cold corner, without kith and kin.

I pick up the phone to call Manasi. It beeps with a message. 'There's an opera tomorrow at Town Hall.' Anger seethes through my brain. I throw the phone on the bed.

23

The Desperate Lover

VATSALA PANDIT
Manhattan, 2015

When regular invitations fail to impress, I try other means.

One day, I appear before him with bright blue highlights in a section of my hair, which makes me look like a hippy. Happily, the mirror tells me that the sudden dash of colour elevates my personality. Shekhar doesn't seem to notice the difference. I try wearing huge accessories on my wrist and neck, things that become hot topics of discussion among my friends in office, but he never utters a word about them all through the session. He doesn't tell me that those are distracting and need to be discarded. Rather, when the neckpieces meddle with the dance movements, I am made to repeat the postures several times till I pluck them out myself and throw them aside to work uninterrupted on the moves.

I wear fluorescent tees and danglers that quite visibly hurt, but all I am discussing with the Dancer are inaccurate hand postures. I appear one day with some bright yellow and red seasonal blooms, expecting to shock him, hoping that he would reprimand me for bringing in meaningless gifts. I want to drag him out of that zone of indifference, in which he stands absolutely undeterred and unmoved, no matter what the other person chooses to do. That day, Shekhar enters late. In a cold harsh voice, he chides me for not starting with the practice.

'For staring across the fence, you don't need my portico. Pray do that without crossing the gates of this guest house,' he hisses.

So taken aback I am with this sudden rudeness that the flowers fall from my hands. No one cares to pick them up.

Then, out of utter desperation, one evening I reach the venue wearing a sexy off-shoulder dress.

Come on, it's New Year Eve! Of course, the snobbish Indian has no plans for the evening. If he does, then it would be some stupid meeting over dinner with some officials whose skin looks like crumpled pumpkin. All my friends are partying. But no point sighing. I am here to receive the characteristic stern look, instead of being at all those lavish parties where delicious cakes would melt in the mouth and wine will flow like a stream. At least today, a diversion from the regular days is due!

May I be destined to ring in the New Year, hand in hand with Shekhar!

I am sure my appearance this evening will finally make him talk. At least he will tell me he won't tolerate my nonsense in his sessions and I need to adhere to the dress code while taking dance lessons. I would then tell him that I am coming directly from a party; I would obviously change into the usual t-shirt I am carrying inside my bag. This would at least pave the path to initiate a conversation. To reason and refute. To say that I was racing my way though, to make it here on time; so I didn't get a chance to change. He would nullify all my excuses one by one. I'll apologize. I'll cry. I'll embarrass him. I'll accuse him of doing this to me on a New Year's Eve when the whole world is celebrating. Then I'll get him to treat me for a coffee to make up for the fiasco. And some cake, maybe?

Yes. This works perfectly. It's fine if it starts with a rebuke, but it has to start. I am tired of waiting. Something has to move to liberate me of this suffocating silence.

This evening Raj Shekhar Subramanian is nowhere to be found!

I leave after waiting for him for four hours. My tears, which flow genuinely out of despair and anger, aren't noticed by anyone.

For the next five days, he remains untraceable. All my phone calls go unanswered. I ask the organizers; they say he is out of station for something important. They would not disclose more. Every evening I sit for three hours at the desolate portico and leave. No one asks anything; no one confirms when he would return. His absence feels insulting but I never leave till I have waited till the last minute.

On the sixth day, he appears again. Without any explanation, he starts removing his shoes. His face carries its trademark austerity as if nothing has happened in between. I watch him for a while and follow suit. My voice chokes, and my eyes fill with tears. Quickly, I wipe them off my face and pull up my hair to tie a knot. Neither of us utter a word about the last few days. Only the mentor knows how severe and merciless he can be when he wants to prove a point. The protégé is left with no option other than silently acknowledging the punishment.

24

The Rise of Krishna

MANASI
MUMBAI, 2015

Blessed with a rich voice and a vast repertoire, Sulochana Gawde was initially trained in Hindustani classical music, before shifting base to Carnatic music as she picked up a strong affinity towards Bharatanatyam. She was a schoolgirl when she met us; now she is a grown-up woman pursuing her post-graduation in history.

Emraan, on the other hand, is not professionally trained in music. He learnt whatever he could after he became a part of Kala Mandir.

Having lost his father at a very young age, Emraan was being raised in a mosque while his mother worked as a cook in several houses to make ends meet. In the mornings, during our practice sessions, he would come and peep in through the window that opened to a room where Bharatanatyam lessons were conducted. Shekhar never sent him away.

Then one day, Shekhar heard him perform the Azan. On enquiring further, he learnt that this was the same boy who trespassed his classes. He also learnt that the boy's interest in his class was more into the rhythm, beats, chants and music that accompanied the physical movements. He was startled to find that Emraan could immediately detect every time a wrong note was played or a dancer missed her footwork to a particular beat. From then on, whenever he stood by the window Shekhar called him inside. In between the classes, Emraan would get up to drink water. He would run straight into my kitchen to grab a bite of whatever was there for breakfast. No one knew when Emraan had become a part of Kala Mandir. No one enrolled him; no one took him through the rules; no one told him the class timings.

Emraan's techniques towards both music and dance were close to perfect. He could recreate the beats of tabla and drums with the ghungroo* tied on his foot with inordinate expertise.

Sulochana has started working on the raga malika that would act as the base for the chants and instrumental music accompanying the performance. Krishna's monologue is being composed predominantly on Raga Bhairav.

Emraan will play Krishna and start the act, so it is more important for him to be in sync with all the supporting performers.

Till late in the evening, Emraan works out his choreography with Ali.

Once again, I catch Sunanda standing at a distance watching him in awe. I look to my left and my eyes meet Varanya's. She is serving tea to everyone. We smile at each other. She takes a cup of tea for herself and sits next to me.

---

*Ghungroo: ornament with bells tied across the ankle for Indian classical dance performances

'Quite a crush she has on Ali,' I whisper.

'If her family knows about this, they'll crush *her*,' Varanya laughs, and so do I.

'What's happening with you and Ali?' I ask.

Varanya shakes her head sadly. 'Nothing yet. Family still livid.'

I am sad to hear this. I too had married an orphan once, but these religious issues did not exist for me. Both my father and husband have led me to the path of spiritualism. Religious negotiations were not a part of our marriage discussions. My father always said, 'All disciplines to reach God are basically philosophies, be it practised in the temple or mosque or church or gurdwara. It's we, humans, who have called these *religions*, so that we can divide ourselves into groups and initiate a battle of superiority with each other.'

Baba was no fundamentalist, but he was a conformist. He ensured that I knew my own philosophical and mythological history to the core.

'Know your history and cultural background so well that no one can get away saying something inappropriate about it,' he used to say. 'And if you are aware of it, you would also realize that every discipline propagates the same beautiful thoughts, and appreciates the same fair deeds. Just that they explain themselves through different stories, worship God with different names, and have different cultural symbols to represent the almighty.'

And Shekhar?

No one knows what his inherited religion is! Jacob Kollipara told me that, when he arrived as a small child in the orphanage, they had baptised him. It was his dance guru, Shri Kritadhi

Iyer, who influenced his dedication towards Shiva and renamed him Raj Shekhar Subramanian. Since then, that is who he is, so much that he didn't ever consider disclosing that part of his life to anyone. Not even me.

In his orphanage, he had grown up with people from all faiths. He probably had more knowledge in each religion's scriptures than that religion's most devout adherents.

I have grown up with such strong foundations of spiritualism, culture and philosophy. Hence it is important for me to maintain a representative correctness about the origin and termination of my act. If I am planning a theme on Kali, I would rather add a logical prelude that justifies the purpose of the Goddess instead of making an abrupt start. So it is only legitimate to have the source introduce his element. It is equally important for Emraan to understand the transcendental connection that leads the charming Krishna to assume the role of the fierce Kali.

Krishna is the purpose; Kali is a medium, to the ultimate destination where souls meet the divine. Kali is a part; Krishna is the whole. Kali is transitional; Krishna is supreme.

Emraan's portrayal of Krishna is conceived with immense confidence, power and authority, conveyed through body language. Each movement of the composition carries a grandeur, as Emraan emotes with the best strengths of his Naatya, putting into use some magnificent facial expressions along with the body that can stretch and bend to create unthinkable postures.

It was Siddharth's idea that Emraan be given double-folded ghungroos for his act, as they would look rich adorning the Lord's feet. It has been one of the best decisions of the team. The moment they are wrapped around Emraan's legs, he complains that it is difficult to move. But soon after, he gets used to them and proposes to bring about an energetic end to his performance where the music centres around him and his footwork. With this powerful beginning, we develop the choreography to its conclusion.

As per our blueprint, at the end of Krishna's act, all the lights of the stage would be turned off for Krishna to disappear and Kali to appear. Kali would start exactly from where Krishna stops, beginning with the same pose with which Krishna leaves the stage.

'When Kali appears,' Natarajan opines, 'there should be a revolving wheel of hands in the background. The wheel would be created by the lights and Kali would stand right at the centre before starting her part.'

After Kali, Shiva would enter and together they would perform the Lasya-Tandava.

25

The Comet Rises

BRIAN HERRETT
Manhattan, 2016

'Consider pushing down the Hudson on whoever has made you this angry. But please don't use a dagger. Cleaning the mess would take too much time,' I say, pulling out a bottle of wine. Shekhar faintly smiles. I give up probing and concentrate on the wine.

I can sense he is enraged about something. He appeared at my flat abruptly today and said he wanted to stay with me for a few days. I am pleasantly surprised. His tense body language tells me there is something beyond the surface reason of us having been friends for so long, which makes him want to begin the New Year with me. I cancel all the parties I had planned to attend and stay back, observing him. He remains absorbed in his laptop, interrupted frequently by phone calls. I am curious, but I must employ other means to find out what has happened.

One of these evenings, I walk into Shekhar's guest house and find Vatsala sitting on the portico, looking absolutely drained.

'Any idea where Shekhar is?' I ask playfully, only to invite the glare of her scornful eyes. 'Would you know?' I ask again.

'Get the hell out of here, pest!' Vatsala snaps.

'I didn't know asking for information is such a terrible offence.' I stand with my hands tucked inside my pocket. I make no attempt to hide my amusement. 'Why do I feel that you did something to make him disappear? Perhaps it was a trick of your witchcraft, and you forgot how to retrieve him?' Giving up all hopes to receive a response, I say, 'Anyway, let me find him out through other sources.'

She looks up, more sober now. I turn to leave. She calls out, 'Hey, sorry about that; I was a bit too disturbed.' I stop.

'How do you know Mr Subramanian?'

I conceal a smile. The girl is pretty smart and focussed. She didn't waste a moment in getting to the point.

'He is a very old friend.' I keep a straight face. 'And you? A student?'

'An associate, and yes I am honing my skills under him.'

I am amused again by the way she avoids the word 'student'. There has to be more to it.

'Brian Herrett.' I extend my hand forward, introducing myself. Vatsala reciprocates. Soon we discover that the organizations we work for have several business deals with each other. Vatsala herself is leading some of these projects. We discuss the long and short of some of them, having found common ground to initiate a conversation. Obviously, I am driven to dig out more information on this sizzling one-sided affair; Vatsala only wants to kill time.

We get up to grab a bite and some coffee from the cafeteria.

As I get up, my bag falls from my shoulders and its contents scatter out into the open. I stoop to pick them up. Vatsala bends down too, but only to pick up a photograph that peeps from beneath some other papers. It is a photograph that captures a moment from Kala Mandir's 'Manipur Stotram', way back in 2005. She looks at me with lots of questions in her eyes. I stretch my hand to take back my possession but she is in no mood to return it.

'You must have seen this on YouTube?'

She nods a yes. 'Not just seen it. I have this memorized moment by moment in my heart.'

'This is one of Manasi's most precious possessions,' I say looking at it, naming the wife deliberately.

Vatsala returns the photograph almost immediately. 'You know her?' she asks.

'Of course I do. She is a charming, warm lady,' I quip, only to find Vatsala turn a little pale. But she recoups quickly.

'Who is his best student in Kala Mandir?' she asks.

'There are two,' I say. 'Shekhar would never admit it, but Ali Iqbal, who played Maya in 'Manipur Stotram', and Varanya Rao, who played the beautiful face of Chitrangada, are very close to him. Not only are these two the oldest members of the troupe, but their relationship with Shekhar is also deeper than just a student-mentor connection. Ali's life mirrors Shekhar's own, as he comes from the same orphanage that Shekhar came from. Ali brought with him not only the competence of a brilliant dancer, but he also helped develop the spirit of sportsmanship within the team.'

I pause to light a smoke. My brain feels lighter with a

puff. 'Varanya's contribution to the team is almost similar, in a different way though. This Andhra girl was a gym instructor. She was trained in Bharatanatyam in her childhood as an extra-curricular activity. She met Shekhar at the gym. Subsequently, she joined him. A lot of issues that raise their head today at the micro-level among the students of Kala Mandir come to Varanya by default. Every time there is a problem, the culprits come to her themselves expecting her to broker peace, afraid that they would be in trouble if things reach Shekhar. Even if they don't, she would know about any unrest between two or more students through sources best known to her and approach them directly to ease tensions with her characteristic compassion and firmness.'

I smile, remembering Ali and Varanya at work. 'Because of these two, minor issues never reach Shekhar or Manasi and they are free to concentrate on more important things. Shekhar is ever grateful to both Ali and Varanya and they are very close to his heart.'

I turn to look at Vatsala. She is taking in my words as if they are scrumptious fodder to her starved soul.

'What did I say that is so interesting?' I ask. My question seems to bring her back to reality.

'No, Brian. I am not asking about his favourite student. I am asking who his *best* student is. Who is the one he can't do without?'

'Manasi,' I say, startling her. 'Manasi was, in fact, his first student. She didn't know a step of Bharatanatyam till she met him.'

I think I saw her eyes turning savage for a few split seconds.

She shrugs, however, and points at her watch, gesturing that it is time to leave. We exchange numbers and disperse.

The next day, I visit her again around the same time.

'You're back, pest?' Vatsala smiles sarcastically, as if she was expecting me. I laugh. This, probably is the usual behaviour of the men that she is accustomed to. People hunt for reasons to come back to her.

This evening, after some inconsequential chit-chat, I drop the bomb.

'He is married and happy, Vatsala. Why are you doing this?' I suddenly ask.

'Who?' she responds innocently.

I don't answer, just sip my coffee. She looks at me for a while, then makes a face. 'I have nothing to do with his marriage.'

'But everyone has a responsibility,' I begin saying, only to be cut short.

'Are you going to advise me on the to-dos and not-to-dos of life? That won't work,' she warns.

'No. Just the curiosity of a journalist, and maybe the concern of a friend. You are treading in difficult waters, Vatsala. From this you will gain nothing but uncertainty and loneliness. Are you sure you want it over a life that can be full of buoyancy and ecstasy?'

She sinks into a dismal silence. Blankly, she looks at the shrubs in the distance.

'I have reached a point of no-return, Brian. I have come too far,' she says with an uncharacteristic calm, certainly not something that comes easily to her. 'I can't detach now even if I wanted to. His silence is far more spiritually rejuvenating than all the activity in my life put together. His demeanour hurts, but there's hope that someday it will soften. If I move away from him, I have nothing; not even that distant hope.'

I am silent. Vatsala watches me for a while and shifts closer. She whispers, almost in my ears, 'What's your secret, Brian? I can sense there's something working in your agile brain. Spill! What's happening up here?' She taps my forehead with her finger, forcing me to smile.

'I want to write the story of his life. I have already started documenting a lot of things,' I venture hesitantly.

'And he doesn't know about this?' Vatsala's eyes widen.

I shrug. If he knew, he wouldn't have offered to stay with me. Vatsala speaks again, bringing me back from my thoughts. 'What would you write about me when you write that story?' she asks teasingly.

'I'd write that there was once a hermit, practising severe austerities in the heart of Manhattan. Just that she was worshipping the wrong god.'

Her smile fades. She stands up, looking for words to explain herself.

'Brian, you won't understand; you just won't! I don't want his home, I want his stage. If we pair up together, he would achieve exponential heights, compared to what anyone else can ever give him. I want to be the first lady in his world of art. I don't really want him to come back to me at the end of every long day, but I want that position of power in all his impending compositions where my act remains pivotal and together we can multiply our contributions to Bharatanatyam…as a couple.'

She stops abruptly, trying to gauge whether I can absorb her urge to achieve the impossible. Restlessly she adds, 'I have come to give him something, Brian; I am not trying to take anything away from him. Maybe he doesn't need it, but it is important for me to give. Till he has taken possession of it, I am not done.' She gasps for air, having spoken too much in the same breath.

She kneels down and faces me, her hard bright determination apparent.

'You know where he is, don't you?'

She waits for a while. I don't utter a single word.

'Did he send you here to discourage me? What did he tell you? When will he return?' she demands.

I waste no further time.

'If you think that Shekhar would ever discuss you with anyone, let alone me, then I am afraid my friend, you have got it all wrong,' I say, perhaps breaking her heart once again. 'I came here because I wanted to tell you, whatever you might want to give Shekhar would be irrelevant to him because he is beyond your capacity to give. His wife once told me that if we can't take away from him his attention-starved childhood and return to him the parents he has never seen, then there is nothing else that we can ever give him. I just thought I should let you know.'

We both sit in silence, resigned and desolate for long, probably giving time to each other to prepare for our respective futures. Just that mine has a visible path; Vatsala's doesn't. The sound of our long deep breathing seems to communicate with each other, even if we say nothing.

That night, I offer to write the biography of Raj Shekhar Subramanian.

Shocked with my sudden proposal, Shekhar thinks I am joking. But I am not. Shekhar says a stern no.

26

The Voice

As much as Shekhar is irritated with Vatsala, he can't be angry for long. Some of her actions remind him of what Manasi did or didn't do to him. Vatsala, of course, is more upfront compared to the latter's characteristic non-aggression. Vatsala demands his attention. Manasi craved for it.

Even today, every time Shekhar comes back home after being away, Manasi flashes a beautiful smile. There is no pretention in that innocent expression that comes naturally to her. Whenever Shekhar's car honks outside, she would let go of all the work in hand and dash to the mirror to check upon her appearance. When nothing looks amiss, and she certifies herself as neither prettier nor uglier than what Shekhar saw her last, she breaks into soft giggles all by herself and runs to receive him from the stairs. Irrespective of any personal low arising occasionally or her physical well-being, she has managed to turn this reaction into a ritual for all these years.

After enduring a long day of corporate drudgery at Britannia Industries, when Shekhar returned late on evenings and began training Manasi, his patience would be running out. At times, he would expect her to pick up things by herself without him having to point out too much. His brain needed to complete a task; his body demanded rest. He would lash out at her when she couldn't comply. Without a word she gathered herself together to work extra hard to satisfy his targets. When they finished, she would bury her face in his chest and cry. She never accused Shekhar of being too fast; she blamed herself for being an awkward learner.

Those memories hurt somewhere very deep inside. Shekhar had moved from one stage of his life to another, and then another, with impossible speed. For him, very single minute was a pursuit. He had walked ahead relentlessly, but at what cost?

Manasi does not bother him with her mischief any longer. Shekhar can't remember when she stopped. Was it after their first show when Shekhar started dealing with the world almost overnight? Yes, maybe. She may have realized then, that burdening Shekhar with having to respond to those innocent ploys would only cause distractions in the grand scheme of things. She may have felt that her wifely tricks no longer had space in her husband's busy schedule. She had probably grown up overnight, as did his popularity. Now Manasi is a woman of poise and elegance, exactly what renowned classical dancer Raj Shekhar Subramanian's wife should be. She is no longer the pampered child from Kolkata, whom I had raised with much love and careful guidance.

I find Shekhar standing on his balcony, pensive and resigned.

'What makes you so sad this evening, son?' my voice speaks, from his subconscious.

'My unavailability for your daughter, Baba, on all the occasions when she may have longed for me to be there for her but never said so. I selfishly chose to close my eyes to anything that made us weak. When she wanted me to spend time with her like every wife does, and I didn't oblige; when she expected me to understand her whims and I ignored; when she may have wished to take a break from the dance routine on romantic rain-washed evenings and I was uncompromising; when full moon nights kept her awake but I fell asleep to attend to something more important on the next day…!'

He sighs. I am quiet as well. Only the monsoon breeze makes its presence felt through the open glass door of his balcony.

'How was she like, Baba, before she became mine?' he asks after a while. I smile.

'She was a notorious scamp. In Chandannagore, she was known for stealing fruits from other people's orchards, but no one could ever catch her. She woke up at unearthly hours to attack mango trees that hung heavy with the fresh fruit of the season, and would sit with her friends preparing pickles out of raw mangoes. Each time she would send a bottle to the owner of the mango tree that she had stolen from. It was her way of enraging them further.'

Shekhar smiles too, trying to imagine little Manasi with two plaits climbing up a mango tree.

'She would disappear from the Chandannagore house at noon when sun was high up in the sky and everyone was sleeping. She stared at the Ganges, made friends with the boatmen, bargained for a free ride on the river, and walked unmindfully on the ghats. She sat for hours on the benches beside the river, trying to make boats from banana leaves, so absorbed in her work that she would not even realize when her slippers got stolen. She'd come back in the evening, barefoot, looking unkempt and dishevelled, and the wrath of all the women in the house would fall on her!'

Shekhar had heard these from her relatives when the couple visited Kolkata after their marriage. Manasi would return shy smiles when he looked at her to confirm the truth of these tales. Today he perhaps senses deeper emotions behind the telling of these stories than mere humour, as he hears them soaked in my affection.

'There is also something about her, that both of us don't know. Something she never shared with you or me, perhaps consciously, or perhaps because she herself isn't sure what it is. But I can sense it. There is something that defines her more than you and I. She derives her strength from there. Find that out, son. I could not put my finger on it in my lifetime. Had I spoken to her about this directly, she would have grown conscious and given it up. This is something you need to understand yourself and stand by her. This is the only challenge my daughter, your wife, has thrown back at us in return of the loyal devotion she has given us her whole life. She'll never say it out loud, but you have to let her fulfil that one desire which drives her very personal fantasies. I could not achieve it, son; promise me that you will not fail her and help her reveal it at some point in her life.'

The last few words are not Shekhar's imagination. I actually said these to him on my death bed, a few hours before I lay still. And Shekhar is yet to relieve my soul by fulfilling this last responsibility I bestowed upon him. It haunts his conscience every time I appear in his subconscious.

Or maybe, I appear because I am still alive to this very personal cause.

27

Arrival of Kali

MANASI
Mumbai, 2016

Arjun Rajawat is in the final year of his degree in architecture. Given his background, I felt it would be easier for him to plan the stage-setting, prepare diagrams and scale models to demonstrate every visual detail. While Arjun is a hard taskmaster with a practical sense of assessing minute details, Dhriti Ganguli is a dreamer from Kolkata. Her heart resides in the works of Tagore and Wordsworth, she was a rank holder in English literature, from Calcutta University. Ganguli-bari* in the Shobhabazar area of North Calcutta has been a staunch patron of art since the British period.

Most of the time, when Dhriti is not studying or rehearsing or reading, she can be found on my terrace. She sits there for hours with her notepad and pen, weaving poetry with her

---

*Bari: Bengali word for home. Ganguli-bari is a traditional term used to denote the home of the Gangulis. Such colloquial terms often become the identities of old ancestral properties in Bengal.

own rhythms and words. Her tranquil dreaminess during those moments irks Arjun. His mind is conditioned to filter every second of life through a massive balance sheet where every action must bring back tangible returns; Dhriti features as a massive liability in the process.

When I nominated them to take over planning the sets and stage, it felt absurd, and I didn't feel too confident. But my heart said it would click.

On this bright Sunday morning Dhriti, Arjun and some others sit together in the hall downstairs. Arjun has finally prepared his blueprint with the timing of the dancers' entries and exits, and all the prop changes along with those of the sets. They explain their plans to Ali and me by drawing lines on the chart; others listen.

Arjun points his pencil on the paper.

'Here, Ali bhai. A part of the stage would be constructed on the lines of the Jagannath temple in Puri. Krishna would emerge from the sea, and present his monologue in the temple premises. The water can be represented with sound and light over the curtain in the background.' He looks at Natarajan, who nods in agreement. Arjun continues, 'The temple needs to be specially constructed though, with thermocol, wood and cardboard.'

Dhriti takes over from here. 'After Krishna's monologue, the background would be darkened and the prop of the Jagannath temple would be removed, only to be replaced by the Dakshineswar temple of Kolkata.'

Natarajan nods again.

In between the discussions, Arjun's phone beeps constantly. He ignores the calls. Everyone looks at him but no one utters a word.

Arjun hands over a file to me. 'We need to share the blueprint with Anna. He can browse through these before we speak to the designers and sponsors in New York to arrange for these. Once the estimates and designs are agreed upon, we'll collaborate and bring it to life.'

I flip through the file, my eyes shining with pride. Our kids have grown up!

Arjun tries to hide a grin as he speaks further, 'You may find some of these ideas very British; very Shakespearean to be precise.' He winks at Sid; they both laugh.

I look at Dhriti; she is giggling too.

Arjun's phone beeps again. He gets serious. Grimly he offers to mail the papers to Shekhar and excuses himself.

I watch him leave; then turn to look at Varanya. 'What's this now?'

'Calls from his home, Akka; they want him to join the celebrations for his first cousin's wedding. But his destination right now is New York, not Udaipur.' She shrugs.

Dhriti butts in, 'I don't understand this. He either avoids those calls or returns monosyllabic responses. I can't imagine behaving like this to my family. I can shout and fight with my folks, but never return a non-response! Arjun is just the opposite. He'll never speak out; he'll sulk and avoid. Why?'

Ali smiles sadly.

'Not everyone is blessed with a family like yours, Dhriti. You guys are educated, liberal and committed to encourage and preserve one's cultural inheritance. Don't compare your Gangulibari's elegance with that of a builder in Udaipur, who has been taught all his life that his only purpose is to multiply money.'

When Arjun came to Mumbai for his schooling, he enrolled for Shekhar's classes without anyone knowing about it. His father tried to intimidate Arjun with threats of disowning him. But Arjun's aspirations were way bigger than his father's.

I sigh and look at my watch. It's time for a Skype call with Shekhar. As much as we employ our brains, Shekhar would still come up with a better idea. He doesn't advise me much on the script. But with the choreography, he is far more stern, creative, perfect! It pains me to see him pushing himself so hard, from another part of the world. Active as ever even after tiring days, his energy seems to belittle all our efforts, hard as we are working. I have sent him all the work that the team has put in, without mentioning that each area is being managed separately by different members. He is yet to give his verdict.

∽

Kali symbolizes spiritual and psychological liberation. She is the archetype of the Great Mother, a protector as well as the destroyer of demonic tendencies. It is said that she protects human beings from their own selves, as she slays the demons of ego and ignorance. The way devotees perceive her depends to some extent on their own levels of consciousness. Her wildness is explained as purely metaphorical. The skulls around her neck represent the letters of the sacred Sanskrit alphabet, and she wears a garland made of hands, representing the severance of the devotee's karma. Kali is the enlightening force that smashes preconceived notions, grants freedom from prejudice and pretentious personal identities. She represents the courage to exhibit oneself unapologetically. She explores the power of truth that often remains hidden behind social masks. So staying in touch with Kali in daily life often means tuning in to that hidden self which one may not have access to ordinarily. She spells a power that can reach beyond the conventional to become bold and fierce—fierce in love, fierce in ecstasy, fierce in the willingness to kill self-bred demons. Freedom is achieved when you are in touch with your soul and are in harmony with your true purpose. In her deepest spiritual essence, Kali epitomizes liberation that demands you become a naked warrior for truth, ruthlessly sacrificing your own pride, ego and other selfish pursuits that captivate you in their limiting materialization. In pointing towards the truth that you have rejected, feared, or ignored about yourself, she inspires constant transformation in your identity over and over again, letting go of the old rigid ideas of who you are, stretching the range of your emotional intelligence, and rediscovering yourself in the process.

My act will start with Kali appearing on top of the stairs. Slowly she will alight to pick up the two lamps kept on the edge of the stage. For fifteen minutes, I will perform with the lamps, the light symbolizing liberation. With the lamps, I will dance elaborating upon the symbols that define the Goddess. The accompanying music will comprise chants of 'Kalika Stuti' from the Kalika Purana and hymns in praise of the Goddess. Sulochana has composed a very potent Kalika Stotram for this based on Raga Bihag; ample use of the mridang will accentuate her vocal genius, giving the composition its desired strength and power.

> The black Goddess keeps the lamps on the floor and bows in front of them into a namaskaram. Soon she

finds herself surrounded by various human weaknesses. Huge crowns to symbolize Pride and Greed; Attachment towards material possessions and Desire to retain them; Lust towards beauty depicted by elaborate floral extravagance; Jealousy of those who lack that beauty; loud body language representing Rage; timid expressions displaying Fear—all these vices dance maliciously across the stage, threatening to assume control over the world. Kali raises her head from the lamps and takes these human evils to task. She dances in fury to protect humans from destructive evils, holding them back from reaching the divine light.

With fast and fierce movements, Kali invites the evils to submit themselves to the earthen lamps. When they pay no heed, she attacks their self-destructive forces, separating the crown from the head to kill Pride and blocks others from rushing towards it to dissolve Greed. While waging war against Kali, pots of wealth fall apart, killing the attachment with temporary possessions. With one stroke she tears off the floral ornaments and ignites spiritual consciousness in them with yogic postures. The Goddess influences Fear and Rage to collide against each other till they are levelled by uniform energy. With wild aggression she intimidates Jealousy and gets the beholder to harmonize with his fellow humans.

With the slaying of each vice, Kali too gives up one aspect of her ferocity. The girdle of hands vanish, her protruding blood-thirsty tongue falls off, the human skulls disappear, her hostility increasingly subsides with each passing moment to be replaced by a newfound tenderness. Defeating those vices bring Kali closer to Shiva. Her darkness is yet another language of desire, her nakedness is the truth with which she approaches her consort, and her being is a vision that never allows the Lord to renounce his resolutions.

At the end of the act, the evils are lifeless. Kali drags them all to the lamps and throws them there, suggesting divine submission and liberation of souls.

Throughout the forty minutes that I would occupy the stage, I would emote the philosophical explanations of Kali's being. My act has been choreographed and rehearsed thoroughly. It is quite final. But somewhere, I feel something is amiss. It feels too predictable; too flat. During rehearsals, the team watches closely to bring in that one moment which can make a difference. They can't find one. But I know what causes me this dissatisfaction. I have always perceived Kali as Shiva's true consort, the ultimate propagator and executor of the cause that he symbolizes. Our composition elaborates upon the purpose of Kali, but doesn't work much on the Lord's corresponding trust and dependence on the Goddess, which unites them like two identities with one soul!

Once again I am back to my study table. Time travels from dusk to dawn in its usual flow, but I am impervious to everything.

28

The Scary Disconnect

VATSALA PANDIT
Manhattan, 2016

When I enter through the entrance of the portico this evening, I stop with a jolt and check my watch. No, I am not late. But then why is he waiting for me here? I study him from head to toe and realize, he is not waiting for me. He is engrossed in some deep thoughts which have nothing to do with me. His eyes are fixed at the eucalyptus forest in the distance, but his mind is exploring something else. Quite unlike the rude indifference that the heartless snob usually wears on his face, today there is a depressing silence. The otherwise dominating, tight-jawed face looks sad today.

Even in this trance, he looks breathtakingly handsome. In a formal blue shirt and beige trousers, hair swept from front to back, hands tucked into pockets, he leans on a pillar with his left leg crossed over his right. The setting sun fills the sky with shades of violet and crimson and orange. His skin shines as light reflects off his fair forehead, moist with perspiration. He must have returned from a meeting and hasn't yet gone upstairs to freshen up. Quietly I put my purse down, grab a few dollars and run out. I walk back a few minutes later with a cup of coffee. I hold it out for Shekhar. He is forced back to the world from which he had taken a sabbatical. His vacant eyes slowly refocus, and he notices the cup, the hand that holds it and then finally, me. His brain remembers the job of the hour; the melancholy disappears.

'I'll be back in five minutes.' He turns to leave, but I am blocking the way already, well-prepared for the reaction my coffee would receive. Without preamble I lift his hand and place the cup within his fingers. Before the grumpy man objects, I take control of the moment. 'Sip the coffee, sir; it's not as harmful as you believe I am to you. Pay me its worth later, if it troubles you too much. While the caffeine elevates your strength, I wish to show you something.'

I feel uncomfortable with the way I am being stared at with a disapproving frown. Those piercing eyes hurt. But if I let that get to me today, I would end up losing an opportunity to impress him. So I keep my face steady, as if Shekhar is just another passing participant in a moment that is solely mine. Swiftly I remove my shoes. I start questioning whatever I am taught for the last couple of months. I show him my research on how celebrated dancers in the past have done the same thing differently; I reveal my study on how different dancers interpreted different emotions and compositions with their own ideologies and how each of them stood out with their specific strengths. I know my knowledge and quest to explore Bharatanatyam from its depth is a rigorous pursuit that would melt the gods. A secret smile touches my insides as he unmindfully sips from the cup.

I exhibit how Kala Mandir has interpreted Lasya and Tandava differently in various compositions and what treatment other dancers have given to it across the years. Soon the Dancer gets talking about the role of Lasya-Tandava not only in Bharatanatyam but also in other forms of Indian classical dance. He speaks about Natya Yoga and Natya Shastra, and the corresponding emergence of Bharatanatyam as an art form originating from the mystic mythological past of India.

'Bharatanatyam was created not just for pleasure of the divine, but to embody cosmic relationships and expressions for all worlds. Hence, it draws inspiration from all activities, be it work or leisure, calm or laughter, war or peace. When Bharata along with the apsaras* and Gandharvs performed Bharatanatyam for Shiva, he asked Maharishi Tandu to develop it further into a Tandava, which later came to mean "masculine" style of dance, and got recognized as the Cosmic Dance of Shiva.'

He sits on the stairs, talking. I interrupt him with several questions. I am not too well-read on Indian mythology. Now that I am getting to know it, I often lose track due to its inherent grandeur. I sit two steps below and demand to know the significance and philosophies behind various mudras, compositions and stories, all of which are getting patiently addressed today.

At some point I ask, 'Why are you so closed to fusion, sir?'

'Because mixing only dilutes the otherwise rich formats of art,' he asserts. 'I understand Bharatanatyam within its strict rules and that's what I choose to practice.'

---

*Apsaras: Celestial beings

'But what if fusion makes the art look even more beautiful? Indian dancers in the past have mixed Bharatanatyam with ballet and offered beautiful compositions to their audience. Haven't you loved those?'

'They may have. But I don't see myself in fusion. Bharatanatyam is beautiful enough if you know how to present it. You don't need mergers to accentuate the beauty.'

'But Sir, aren't you being too rigid? Doesn't rigidity limit the scope of art? Fusion is celebrated worldwide! To create fusion you have to know extremely well all that you are trying to fuse,' I argue.

He smiles.

'There is no logically appropriate answer to what you've asked, Vatsala. It is my choice not to club Bharatanatyam with anything else. It is as pure as my faith—just like the relationship of a mother and child. I can't split it between anything else. Just like a mother doesn't need to accentuate her beauty to come to her child, I feel Bharatanatyam is an extremely self-sufficient dance form, the beauty of which only increases the more you explore it within its boundaries.'

I keep telling him about my own ambitions with Bharatanatyam, how I want to take myself forward with Kala Mandir and what a dream it is for me to perform on stage with Shekhar and his troupe. I add 'and his troupe' cautiously to ensure that he is not put off. But I can see that he is only half-listening. Had he been more conscious about this moment, he probably would have left by now putting an end to my ramblings. I try my best to engage him in a conversation, even if he is a passive participant to this strange intimacy. I tell him

I want to learn enough from the austere Dancer so that one day I can return to him a composition that I solely spearhead and execute. Someday, the maestro would dance to an act choreographed by me.

He is inexplicably pensive and disconnected. I am not sure where it originates from. I want to reach out, but he wouldn't tell me even if I ask. And getting him conscious would be suicidal. I am sure it's not me that bothers him this evening. There is something else to it. I have touched deep inside Shekhar with my research on the art. The doubts that he may have nurtured regarding my sincerity must have evaporated considerably. Yet, he is treating me with an intervening indifference which he refuses to let go off.

There is something here that belongs to me, which this man has kept with himself. I can't rescue it, because I don't quite know what it is. Every time I see him, it feels even more apparent. And the high-headed hunk loves to play difficult, dangling it right in front but not allowing me the satisfaction of complete experience. With all my determination I want to own what is rightfully mine. And every time he leaves, I feel that obscure treasure going away with him with an assurance to never return.

This evening when we are done, I pick my purse but can't bring myself to leave. The darkness of the night is dispelled by the beautiful moon shining bright above. Shekhar still sits on the stairs with his back towards me, assuming I am gone. One of his legs is on the stairs; the other lifted close to his chest and bent at the knee, where he rests his left hand. The right hand hangs loose, seemingly as disowned as he is at this moment. The dim light of the portico doesn't do much to enliven the silence of the place. Nothing other than the occasional deep breaths of the Dancer can be heard. God knows how long he stays like that. I almost stop myself from blinking, afraid that the slightest distraction would bring him out of the spell. I even try to hold back from inhaling too frequently. The hunger pangs that erupt after the sessions are also at rest tonight.

After a long time, he turns abruptly. And he spots me sitting quietly behind.

Almost as a reflex, I get up as well. With slow steps, I start moving backwards to avoid the obvious confrontation that is to follow, as he walks towards me. I don't need light to read the disgust on his face. The next few moments are going to be difficult. I try to gather up my thoughts to explain myself, but my brain feels dysfunctional. I mutter a curse.

Shekhar utters something. Almost hypnotized by his cruel eyes upon me, I am not sure I hear him. My insides shudder; he looks tired and his vision is probing too deep, making it impossible for me to put up any mask that can shield my fondness for him. I look away and wait, my lungs feel out of breath and my throat hurts.

If only he would hug me tight right now, sheltering me with the warmth of his chest and reassure me that I am at least allowed to feel concerned. But all that he has to offer is a dispassionate command.

29

A Call to the Cosmos

RAJ SHEKHAR SUBRAMANIAN
Manhattan, 2016

No one ever questions my decisions. They just follow.

Initially I never encouraged individual opinions, because I had to build an empire single-handedly, without any resistance from my own circuit. Moreover, Manasi never asked me anything; she accepted my words as an absolute command. Had Manasi been here, she would have disempowered Vatsala too from asking so much about my choices.

Or would she?

For a split second it occurs to me, did Manasi ever have a substantial query which I overlooked? Why can't Manasi ever have a different vision over a composition? Does she nurture her own creative ambitions? Having danced all her life as I wanted, is dreaming of a stage where *I* dance to fulfil *her* fantasies too unreasonable?

I feel weak and shaken. In my ruthless journey I never stopped to look around. I didn't have the luxury of time, or maybe I never cared.

I have been discussing the upcoming show with Manasi. I like her concept. From whatever I have been told in detail, and from what she has mailed, I have been evaluating the script and choreography very critically. I have dissected in my brain, each and every moment of the dance that would go up for the show. Long conversations over phone and Skype have helped to hold the strings tight and ensure that preparations are going right. But on this isolated evening, I feel like retiring. For the first time in all these days, I feel relieved to have given Manasi the freedom to conceptualize her own show for the inauguration of Kala Mandir in New York.

From now on though, I would keep my involvement to a bare minimum. I won't interfere unless required. Manasi has sent me some files to be verified. These carry the planning details which must be whetted and processed. But I won't advise any modifications to those. I'll just follow Manasi's instincts through this composition and do as I am told. The show should throw up a lot of what burdens my brain with mysterious allegations.

Feeling slightly more settled, I get up. I turn and find Vatsala sitting behind. Her session has ended long back. What the hell is she doing here then? I walk towards her; she takes slow steps behind.

'What brings you back here?' I demand to know.

She cooks up a story. 'I forgot my purse, so came here to take it back.' Her voice sinks.

I walk past her; the girl follows me. As we reach the reception, she plays a new game.

'Sir,' she calls from behind.

I stop, but refuse to look at her.

'You looked so abandoned!'

I start walking again. Just when I turn to take the lift, Vatsala cries out desperately from behind. 'What is my fault, sir? What have I done to receive this insulting indifference from you? Why do I have to live with the fear of being disowned any moment?'

She gasps for breath, not sure of what she is complaining about. God knows what reassurance she is looking for. I turn to rest my eyes coldly on her.

'It is already quite late, Vatsala. Leave right now if you wish to come back tomorrow.'

And I walk straight up the stairs without looking back.

'What is my fault!'

The question hovers around my brain, causing a never-ending restlessness all through the night. Every particle of my consciousness echoes in that question, for which I don't have an answer. Manasi, my wife of seventeen years, has never asked me this.

It has been years since we met with that terrible accident. We were driving back from Pune to Mumbai. I was at the steering wheel, when I suddenly suffered a blackout. The car crashed against a tree. Before I fainted, I heard Manasi scream in pain, crying for help. I still remember that voice, just before my senses faded. The helpless tension she must have experienced all alone still rips apart my heart.

The doctors declared that Manasi will never be a mother. Her uterus will not be able to take that pressure because it has suffered beyond repair.

Not that we had any immediate plans of starting a family.

The thought of a child wasn't anywhere in my mind. But Manasi wanted to be a mother. As usual, she never expressed what she felt. I saw it in her eyes nevertheless, when I was fit enough to be updated about the developments. I felt devastated. My first gift to my wife was an ill-fated disability!

While I sank into the dark of helpless despair, Manasi dealt with the grief and loss all by herself. She took me to task, as depression towered over my life like a tall amorphous shadow. With enormous strength she pulled herself back, waiting patiently for me to overcome my suffering. Never did she even remotely express any contempt towards me, or life, or even God.

I took a long time to accept that there was no way I could bring back what was already lost. I dived into work with a vengeance, while Manasi dived into me with all her energy. I could never forgive myself for being at the wheel on that fateful evening. Manasi behaved as if the accident never happened.

Her conviction towards dismissing that evening as non-existent is so strong that at times I too feel that it was no more than a passing nightmare. The guilt, though, comes back to me with its claws drawn whenever I think that Manasi cannot be a mother because I let her down.

Nothing irks more than a cruel, ill-fated joke. I came to this earth without any celebratory introduction; and I'll have to leave without a formal conclusion. I was born an orphan, and I will have to die childless.

Today, I remember the day once again because fourteen years ago it was the same evening when I lay unconscious, unable to share with Manasi the physical pain that she was going through. I couldn't support her; I couldn't protect her.

I sit up on the bed to look outside the window. A beautiful moonlit path with trees on both sides presents itself before my eyes. I know that Manasi too hasn't forgotten this day. But even in my absence she would not indulge herself so far as to recall those ghastly images from the past.

At 3 a.m., gallons of water flow down my throat as I reach for the phone. It is about time that Manasi comes here and kills the loneliness of my nights. Things are almost set. My rehearsals with the team should also begin. The show is not far away; everyone needs to get accustomed to things. The dancers need time to comprehend what they should take extra precautions against, given that the audience here would be NRIs and Americans. The purpose is to lure them to join Kala Mandir as students.

The impatience that reflects in my voice tonight is not something that the person on the other side of the phone is accustomed to.

30

The Dance of Desire

MANASI
Mumbai, 2016

I search deep within myself to find a suitable progression to the act. Instead of Shiva appearing on his own after Kali has killed the demons, it would work better if the Goddess invokes the Lord to come to her. Yes, that would be a legitimate advance to be made by the divine woman, who represents Shiva's purpose in her being and takes it upon herself to execute his task of cleansing and renewing lives. For the next few minutes of the act, I weave the tale of Kali's desire for the Lord, who charmed her into transforming from a Goddess to a woman!

THE DANCE OF DESIRE

> Kali is no longer the destructive force that threatens and intimidates. Her body thrilling, eyes playful, footsteps coy, strands of her hair entangled between long fingers, she walks sensuously following the beats

of the damru* to be united with her sacred companion. Through luscious movements and aesthetic postures, the woman desires to submit and seek submission in turn from the man who rules her mind, heart and soul. She emotes in isolation, revealing tenderness and desire, as she calls for Shiva.

Far away, amidst the pounding resonation of the damru, Shiva opens his eyes.

Rasia!

That's what would be a befitting title for the show. The tale of the ultimate seductress who aspires to recast the hermit, Shiva, into a pleasure-seeker, Rasia.

This is the woman who the world had called furious, scary, terrible. Those bloodshot red eyes, blood-stained lips and armed hands are now prepared to be reintroduced as Mahamaya, the magnificent illusion. Her soul conspires to ignite divine passion within the heart of the ascetic, inviting him out of his detachment. She doesn't seek to charm the Lord with the beauty of her body; she offers to unite with him in a space that is cleansed, virtuous and free of falsehood and hypocrisy. She creates 'home' for the Lord, ensconcing him into hearts that are free from deceit. The more she liberates, the greater her beauty and elegance magnifies. Fulfilling the purpose of the God is her only tool to seduce him from being a recluse to Rasia!

---

*Damru: small two-sided drum played by Shiva

Together, Shiva and Kali would perform Lasya-Tandava indulging themselves further in the *Dance of Desire*.

Rasia would also be my subtle declaration to the world, precisely Shekhar, all those thoughts and beliefs that I have nurtured secretly, to protect the austere sincerity with which I pursued them. In Kali, I have always found the most unadulterated disposition of womanhood.

Early next morning, I request updates from the group on the progress they have made so far.

An engineer, the soft-spoken Natarajan Iyengar understands the interplay of lights and the effects they are capable of creating if mixed and matched correctly. However, his expertise is contained because he fails to think of anything above average. His creative strength is his Manipuri wife, Tashi, who tags along with him on many days as if she has always been here.

Tashi is the only one at Kala Mandir who is not a trained Bharatanatyam dancer. She runs an NGO called Nirvaan that aims to empower impoverished women by training them in various arts and handicrafts, so that they find the means to sustain themselves. They mostly make things for home décor, using mirrors and glass to reflect and refract light through them in a way that the rooms which they adorn look lively.

Natarajan opens a map. Everyone gathers around to hear his plan.

He explains, 'These are the stage measurements, as provided by Anna. Kali's *Dance of Desire* will have red lights illuminating the top of the stairs and the temple as the backdrop. With the beat of the mridang, the lights will subsequently illuminate other parts of the stairs and the background as well. Soon, soft yellow and blue lights from above will further accentuate Kali's facial and physical expressions.' He looks at Tashi, and she elaborates further, saying, 'I will have the props arranged and delivered from Nirvaan. When Natarajan came to me with his ideas on lights and props, the first thing that came to my mind was, why not associate Nirvaan as one of the creative partners for the show? The entire job of creating the props, items of stage-décor, architectural props and of course, light, could be outsourced to Nirvaan. Yes, the risks are huge, but by doing this, Kala Mandir would make a bold social statement. What do you think?'

I almost shout in excitement, 'Brilliant. We'll go ahead with this.'

Natarajan responds happily, 'Great, then. I have discussed with Arjun, Dhriti and Sid, and we have reshuffled our plans. With Tashi coming in as a partner, we know we'll get exactly what we want. Sid has already given her the colours and designs.'

Sid confirms this with a nod.

Dhriti clarifies some more, 'We have decided to have brass bells and beautiful lanterns hanging from above at different parts of the stage. Artificial winds would swing them to and fro to add depth to the ambience, especially when energetic performances take place. From the sides, the walls will have conical torches where fire would be replicated with fine cloth swaying rapidly as air passes through it at a very high speed, and orange light would illuminate the cones and the cloth. This torch idea is solely mine.'

She emphasizes on the 'mine', looking at Arjun with a sarcastic smile. He ignores her. 'With props like this, a light and shade effect would be generated, so that when dancers exhibit their passionate best, their shadows would echo their movements from multiple angles enhancing the visual experience of the audience. Tashi will bring the samples of the torches, bells and lanterns for approval.'

Natarajan adds, 'These metal props with mirror and sequin work on them would be exposed to light falling upon them from strategic angles, directly from above or softly from the sides, to heighten the desired effect.'

'We will be in New York next month,' I announce finally and the group erupts in a cheer. This journey is going to be special for everyone.

Kala Mandir is all geared up for the inaugural show. The days are ablaze with activities. I have provided explicit details of each of my plans to Shekhar. They didn't come back with his input or instructions. This is a little surprising. Shekhar will join the rehearsals when we reach New York.

With a storm in my heart, I have been waiting to face Shekhar. Till date he hasn't asked me how I came up with this concept. He hasn't probed to understand why I never voiced these thoughts to him before. Even when I insist that he takes updates from Sid or Arjun or Emraan over Skype, he doesn't question why! Patiently he listens, with his conversations strangely focused only on what needs to be moved from his end at New York to facilitate our progress. And then he hangs up. That's quite unlike him.

Shekhar had mentioned that in the evenings, he tutors an NRI girl in Bharatanatyam. Though pronounced with a weird coldness, Shekhar said that the girl is rather strange, but her grasp on the art is spectacularly deep and that she is truly creative and talented.

I smile. It is good that he has found himself a student there. Nothing defines him better than his students. He finds profound joy in their company. I look back at the dancers of Kala Mandir, running around enthusiastically putting things together for the show. Each student here is a live representation of his achievements. They portray the picture of a collective future that originated from him. Shekhar often says that his students will take his vision further when he will be no more; they will keep him alive long after his last breath on the planet.

It is great news that Kala Mandir already has its first student in New York. This girl, blessed with Shekhar's mentorship and individual attention while tuning her skills, is truly lucky.

I remember my own solitary evenings with Shekhar.

Being his first student, who knows better than I, that no one will be able to take from him the art that he had once bestowed upon me? Those days his approach was rugged, expectations unpolished. But the grit with which he taught was undiluted, free from the multiple horizons he has to manage today. All his attention then, day and night, had been with me. Even in his office, between work, he thought of me and designed new ways for me to pick up skills fast and with finesse. As much as it aided me in transforming from a novice to a fine artiste, it simultaneously laid the foundation of our relationship. It was because of Shekhar's purest gift to me, that today I can come up with something that voices my own truth back to him.

He sounds different of late!

My wandering mind stops abruptly. Something is amiss

somewhere. Coincidentally, the phone vibrates and Shekhar's face flashes on the screen. I smile and take the call, walking upstairs to avoid the chaos around.

∽

Twilight is setting in as I stand alone on the terrace with my phone in my hand. Our conversation was as usual, yet it feels disturbing. I look at the phone again.

He never talks like this. How is that today he has the time to look back at his past? Since when did he start caring about things that have been left behind? Something is wrong with him these days. He speaks softly and slowly, and hears each of my responses with minute attention, never interrupting in between. The show is drawing closer. This is the time when Shekhar should be brimming with energy. Every moment he should be coming up with some genius idea that sets an example. Why is he still so quiet?

The adjoining houses are lighting up one by one. The sea looks restrained and lifeless. I frown looking at the vast expanse of water.

Is he too lonely there? Is he following a very demanding schedule? Does he need me with him now?

No!

The very next moment I dismiss the logic. Shekhar doesn't need anyone. Not when it is Bharatanatyam. He's complete by himself in that space. He is our one-man army. It's we who revolve around him in invisible orbits, because without him we are lost. Shekhar is too proud to lose his vitality to such silly issues. On any given day, he is capable of disowning everything that he has achieved and restart his journey from scratch.

But then, what is it? I turn and walk along the railing of the terrace, discussing various possibilities in my mind. And I stop.

What is the date today?

Just once, after a dreadful accident that took away much more than it should have, had I seen Shekhar completely devastated. He blamed himself for that which was gone. He still does. I have thrown the day out of my calendar, cremating it somewhere in the past. But it is the one ruin that Shekhar still goes back to from time to time.

Is it the accident? Again? Is he caught up in the same depression? No. Not now. This is not the time. I shudder, unable to dismiss the possibility as just a vain unsettling assumption.

I wish I could reach out to Shekhar right now.

31

A New Beginning

VATSALA PANDIT
Manhattan, 2016

This evening when I reach the guest house, for a moment I feel I have entered the wrong building. The spacious lounge in front of the reception that is usually deserted is today overflowing with people. Some are sitting on the floor in groups, discussing something seemingly urgent, many others are running around the place trying to arrange this and that, and even the dark stairs that go up to Shekhar's room finds its privacy violated by frequent intruders going up and coming down in haste. The lift is forever occupied. All lights everywhere are turned on; voices chirrup and order and growl from all corners. Even the ever-sleepy receptionist, who works in slow motion when awake and returns only a retarded look when a query is addressed to her, seems to have taken steroids to bring herself alive.

Suddenly, this isolated house situated in one corner of a boring lane brims with noise and colour.

I am the only one unhappy here, looking around irritated with these developments. So many people here means an interference into the few hours this man spends with me every evening. He is already quite a tough nut to crack, who won't waste a minute to consider that his student expects more from him than simply teaching her Bharatanatyam; these distractions are further hurdles in my way. I take a turn to reach the portico and stand there astonished.

A group of dancers are practising their steps in unison while a trainer supervises them. I look around for Shekhar but he is nowhere to be found. There's Brian Herrett walking around leisurely, with a large bag hanging from his shoulders. I reach out to him, grab him by his shirt and pull him towards me a bit too harshly. Though unprepared, Herrett doesn't look offended by the sudden attack.

'What's the plan, baby?' he flirts.

I ignore his tone, 'What's happening here? Who are they? What are you doing with them?'

'The Kala Mandir team, obviously.' Brian looks surprised. 'Surely you weren't expecting that only you and Shekhar will take over the stage for the inaugural function!'

The opening show! The sudden commotion and crowd begin to make sense to me now. This is Raj Shekhar Subramanian's group from India. They are rehearsing for the opening show. I had completely forgotten about it, happily spending some fantasy evenings in his company. So foolish of me to feel that these evenings would never cease and that I have all the time in the world to take it slow, enjoying whatever morsels of his benevolence he extended towards me.

Enjoy or get depressed?

Anger erupts inside my brain like molten lava. They threaten to come out as tears.

'Hey! Is everything alright?' Brian asks.

'The damn inaugural function,' I mutter, looking around angrily at the dancers. 'Because of some tight deadlines at work, I could not remain in touch with the organizers lately. I had no clue of what was happening here. And no one bothered to inform me about new developments.'

I look at Brian as if he is responsible for everything. 'Yes, it's true that I remained unavailable for a while, but that certainly didn't mean I have given up on my stake in all of this. I am one of the chief volunteers for the event, dammit!'

My voice rises with every word. Some of the dancers even glance this way. Brian holds me tightly by the arm and drags me to a corner of the cafeteria, relatively vacant at this hour. I don't know whether I actually walk there, or he has to carry me.

'I have even used my personal savings to conduct those road shows raising awareness on Bharatanatyam; many have come on board only because of my persuasion,' I say, my eyes red with hurt and unshed tears. The only comfort I have is another pair of eyes that seem sympathetic and a soul who is patient enough to hear me out.

'I have used official contacts to approach them, putting to risk my reputation at work. I would be in a lot of trouble had this been found out. Does anyone here have slightest respect for any of my efforts?'

Brian perches on a table and lights a cigarette. The smoke he puffs out is as dirty as the crowd here this evening.

'Is he really a man? Or does he just use his arrogance to hide his impotence?'

At this, Brian looks back at me. The friendly, sympathetic eyes have grown hard. They advise silently that I have gone too far; I should stop. I curse and run away, leaving him alone.

Hastily I walk to a corner and flip open my phone to dial a number. As I begin to give a piece of my mind to a member of the organizing committee across the phone, I am curtly cut short and informed that no one has the time to accommodate 'stories' and anyone is liable to be replaced by the best available substitute if they are unavailable without prior intimation. I am also reminded of the many messages that were sent, trying to get in touch with me regarding my whereabouts; my non-response towards them has prompted the organizers to put me on the back-burner. The phone goes dead.

I curse again.

All this while I was under the impression that getting tutored by Raj Shekhar Subramanian himself would fetch some unspoken perks. Of course, the Dancer has passed on no such instructions; neither would he care to intervene and sort anything for me now.

Heart burning with rage, I walk back fast through the same path and gasp as I am abruptly stopped at the elevator. A young guy stands blocking my way. He asks what business I have upstairs. With enormous restraint, I hold back from slapping him hard. He is probably still in his teens, behaving as if he owns the place.

'Stay the size of your boots, dude.'

'Just because you are wearing a pair too, lady, you can't just take yourself anywhere,' he snaps back sarcastically.

I try to dismiss him but surprisingly the boy behaves like he is another version of Shekhar. His facial muscles reflect the same gestures that speak of a sense of absolute and ruthless command, paired with a general disdain for everyone.

'Why are you people so possessive as if each one here is a property of the other?' I say despairingly. I flash my Volunteer Card and push him aside. In a short while I am rushing through the second floor. I halt only when I have turned the knob of the door and entered without permission. He isn't there. Three women stare back at me. Softly I mumble an apology, trying to move out unobtrusively, when one of them stops me.

'You must be Vatsala,' she smiles. 'Nice to see that you are a part of us already.'

We exchange pleasantries. I enquire about Raj Shekhar Subramanian with all the politeness I can muster.

Manasi does not know when he would return. She invites me to sit with her over some homemade delicacies she has brought from India. Of course, I am in no mood for these over-friendly gestures from the wife of the person who has always considered my presence to be an obstacle to his private evenings. But I can't behave rudely and storm out either, as much as I want to. Anger rips apart my veins. But this day is not going too well for me. I need to watch out so that my temper causes no further damage. I remain cordial to Manasi, observing her with an eagle eye.

So mediocre and outdated! What does this woman have in her to hold Shekhar's attention to the extent that it doesn't deviate even in her absence? I feel bitter. Soon, I can bear it no longer and I rise to leave. I am about to open the door, when he enters. 'What are you doing here? I was waiting downstairs,' he asks surprised.

'I was there a while ago. You hadn't arrived yet and some people were practising. I came upstairs to look for you and met Manasi here,' I respond calmly.

The stone-hearted man doesn't have time for my clarifications. He leaves the room with me following him in haste, thankful that my trials with Manasi are over for the day.

'Listen, I won't be available for teaching you regularly for a while now,' he says as we reach the lounge, his eyes looking around to survey all the areas he will have to involve himself in by cutting me out. 'The show is just three months away and I have to get going with the rehearsals. A lot has to be arranged here. I shall set you up with Ali or Dhriti. Come, I'll introduce…'

'No,' I interrupt loudly. Shocked, he turns and looks at me.

'No,' I repeat, this time more controlled. Tears fill my eyes. My voice sounds hoarse as I speak. 'No one in your team has the capacity to teach me, sir, because I am better than all of them. And don't shut me up today, because you know that what I am saying is not arrogance. It is the truth.'

I wipe my face with my hands and speak again. 'You haven't been spending all those hours with me because of a stupid challenge I threw at you in the beginning. I know that as much as you do. After long chaotic days you continued to teach me because I deserved every bit of it. You didn't do me a favour. So, I won't, either. If I continue with Bharatanatyam, I will learn it only from you. Otherwise, I give it up right here and no one will ever know I had any bit of it within me.'

I hold my breath, waiting to hear the final words of dismissal.

32

The Negotiation

RAJ SHEKHAR SUBRAMANIAN
Manhattan, 2016

This day had started on a different note. I was just back from some meetings when Sid dragged me to a secluded corner of the first floor.

'What now?' I asked the young rebel impatiently.

'Anna,' he wiped his forehead with a tissue. 'For a year now I have been interning at a design house in Mumbai. Akka may have told you about it.'

I remembered talking to Varanya and Manasi about it long back. Fickle interests and this drive to earn money could be threatening for Kala Mandir. Manasi was livid. Yet, I had instructed them not to stop Sid.

'Why did you do that?' I asked. 'You needed money?'

'No. Their work is fun. I wanted to learn a bit,' he tried to explain. I smiled.

'Promise me, that from now on you won't hide things. If you are not doing anything wrong, then you don't really need to lie or hide. Have the patience and conviction to convince others. It helps in building trust.'

I tried to leave. I could see Vatsala frantically looking for me downstairs; she said something to Brian very rudely. How do these two know each other? Perhaps I needed to intervene. But I was stopped again.

Sid had bent down to touch my feet and held out a packet towards me. I frowned.

'Anna, these are my savings. I was wondering if we need this now…' He couldn't complete his sentence. After standing speechless for a moment, I touched the packet gently, feeling love in its purest form under my palm, before pushing it back. I hugged him.

I sent him off saying I would ask for it if I required money. He sped away.

This is how rewarding the job of a teacher is. These boys and girls are my confidence, my pride, my present and my future. I won't ever let them walk away from me.

But I can't stand apart for long, mulling over Sid. Vatsala isn't visible any longer. I take long strides to check what is happening downstairs.

I confront her a short while later, receiving an ultimatum like no one has ever dared to give me before.

Silently, I pick up a bottle of mineral water lying next to me and hold it out to her. She opens the bottle in haste and gulps it down with an urgency to soothe more than her throat.

Her face is angry, eyes still wet, she hiccups a little because of the sudden rush of tears. She looks like a silly little girl who has always stood first in class but this time her trophy has been taken by someone else.

The fact that she is a rare talent is certainly the truth. Of course, I don't believe she has any plans to give up. But artistes are sentimental fools. When they are hurt in places that matter most, they sometimes get self-destructive. That is a concern for this woman too.

When she is calmer, I offer her to observe the rehearsals and practise with the group for the next few days.

'My rehearsals must go on. There is not much I can do about it. But you can come down any time and spend as much time as you choose to, so that your learning doesn't stagnate. Keep your experiences multiplying as you tag along with the team to witness what happens before and during a show. Just ensure that nothing is disturbed by your presence. I don't want any drama here.'

Vatsala opens her mouth again to say something; I stop her with a raised hand. 'There will be no further discussion. Whether you come or you leave, is your call now.' I gesture for her to leave.

Vatsala stares mutely for a while. Her aggression has turned unexpectedly pale and the usual spark in her eyes is gone. She turns and leaves. I stand there watching her go. With slow steps, exuding the remorse of losing a secret war, she walks off.

With a tinge of sadness, I wait until I can see her no more. She has more to lose in the days to come. Vatsala is dangerously walking towards nothing, blissfully ignorant that the object of her desire does not really exist. She is hopelessly headed towards a trap, the depths of which will take her down into a bottomless trench. The Raj Shekhar Subramanian she claims to be in love with is a tireless, staunch worshipper seeking and deriving selfish pleasure from practising Bharatanatyam; he is not capable of being anyone's lover. If he could, he would have been that for his wife.

That's where today I feel I have disappointed myself. The world applauds my credentials as a dancer, teacher, a visionary, a human being; God knows what myriad flattering adjectives they use. They aren't informed that in my carefully constructed success, I have walked over the one who has always stood by me in all sincerity.

I have used Manasi but have given her nothing in return.

33

The Leopard's Focus

BRIAN HERRETT
Manhattan, 2016

This wasn't something I hadn't seen coming. Yet, the only comfort I can offer to the juvenile girl is giving her a patient ear and allowing her to spill everything from her heart uninterrupted; so what if she is condemning a friend whom I have known for years. I know that Vatsala has brought this upon herself. But still, I feel sad for her. What do I blame her for? That she is in love with Shekhar? Everybody loves him. It is only that this woman is passionate about it. She wants a public acknowledgement of his affections in a place that is a temple for Shekhar—the stage.

In her madness to prove a point and bring him to New York with an opportunity which he couldn't decline, she hasn't left a single stone unturned, breaking every barrier with a desperate strength. Her mission to get unconditional access to Shekhar was never fulfilled; neither could she get him to return the slightest fondness in return for all her dedication. But at least he was spending time with her. The arrival of his dance troupe came to her as a rude shock, taking away whatever little she had been holding on to.

I indulge her for a while, listening to her rant. But eventually I give up. If I don't stop her, her vulgarity will only increase. Not only is Shekhar a dear friend, but I am also close to his family and troupe. Most importantly, I respect him too much to allow someone talk so coarsely about him.

She runs away sensing my resistance. I follow her, wary of what she would do next. I witness her conversation with Shekhar. I am surprised as Shekhar offers her a bottle of water. She is shocked too by this sudden kindness. She snatches it from him, perhaps fearing that it will disappear if she blinks. I hear Shekhar dismissing her after he pronounces his terms.

Vatsala walks aimlessly for a while. I walk behind her in silence. She finds herself still holding close to her chest, the bottle of mineral water that Shekhar had given her. Angrily she throws it in the next dustbin she encounters on the way, and stops to sit down on a bench near the Hudson River. The moisture laden breeze cuts through her skin. She is shivering. I approach her and place a hand on her shoulder. She turns and throws herself at me, sobbing. I wait for her to calm down.

'Try to think straight. Prepare a list of what you are going to do for the next few hours,' I advise a few minutes later.

'I need to eat something before my brain melts off. I have the worst migraine!' she confesses and pops a pill. 'Then I'll head towards the Department of Cultural Affairs to talk to the organizers about renewing my volunteership.'

'Keep calm all through, even if the officials' comments are against your tastes,' I advise again. She tries to smile.

For the next few days Vatsala operates like a machine. From

work, she comes straight to the workshops of Kala Mandir. She sits there watching them rehearse and debate and improve with each passing moment. No one objects to her presence. Soon she befriends some of the people. Quietly she eats the food served for the dancers.

Astonished with the hidden facets of this woman, I keep observing her. I can't say I am not attracted. But I keep my fascination to myself. By now she knows each of the roles by heart. She has started appearing as a proxy if any dancer is caught up with something else. She even helps some of them gain perfection with their postures and people are open to learning from her.

The only exception is Siddharth, who continues to remain cold towards her.

As she sits watching the rehearsals, Sid stands apart, scrutinizing her shrewdly. I appear from behind and pat him on his head.

'Don't even try. She's too old and ill-tempered for you,' I tease him.

Sid laughs sarcastically. 'Huh! Not even over my dead body.'

I settle down beside him with a coffee. Sid moves his eyes from her and whispers, 'This woman looks like devil. Why does Anna encourage her?'

I smile at his disgust. 'Don't you worry, your Anna knows better.'

'Of course he knows better,' Sid lashes out. 'And I know who he is doing a favour to. God knows how you tolerate her.'

He walks away briskly, leaving me shocked. But Kala Mandir isn't as blind as Shekhar and Manasi pretend to be. I can't blame them for the assumptions they have made. Quietly, I get up to take my seat beside Vatsala.

The feisty girl watches the entire composition over and over again, observing Shekhar, Manasi and rest of the group rehearsing the act in minute detail. She speaks softly so as to make it audible only to me, but I guess what she says is meant for herself.

'His biggest strength is his wife? No!'

She looks at me, but expects no response. 'She holds the reins of Kala Mandir exactly the way he wants it. Doesn't she have a life of her own?'

She bends further towards me. 'What about her individuality? In that large bindi, the cotton saris, the long hair, the bangles in her hands, and following his orders with such minute precision, Manasi practically announces that she is Raj Shekhar Subramanian's wife and nothing else,' Vatsala says with contempt.

'So you think she must claim to be my wife?' I ask with a straight face. She turns to slap the back of my head.

'No, duffer. You know what I mean.' She grins. 'I can never think of reducing myself to be the mere extension of someone else.' She pauses. 'I want a lot from life, and I want to give back to life an equivalent vastness. I can't be anyone's shadow. You understand?'

She looks at me, trying to gauge how far I have comprehended her thoughts. 'Come on now. My presence is meant to illuminate further the person who stands beside me,' she states arrogantly.

'I want people to appreciate my looks, my presence; but more importantly, I want to appreciate myself when I look into the mirror every morning. Each day I try to look, feel and act different, exploring my versatility. I experiment with myself to understand the range that defines me. Each day I make a conscious attempt to extend that range. Those experiments give me enormous pleasure. I can love myself like no one ever would.'

I exhibit no emotion either in support or against whatever she means.

'What never fails to surprise me is that Shekhar is never intrigued by my freshness!' We look at each other.

'Manasi's stagnancy is all he stays occupied with.' She stops to look at Shekhar, and turns to me again. 'With me, he could have experienced the pleasure of living with many women, each of whom is different from the other. I am cool, patient, stubborn, loving, passionate, restless and delightful, and every passing day I am a different woman with something new about me that my lovers in the past raved about. But hopelessly, this man is caught up in a boring predictability that can only boast of its steady rhythmless poise. It shows no signs of phasing out with time!'

She loses the flow of her monologue as she is interrupted by a loud click. She turns and finds me smiling with the camera pointed at her.

'What the…!' She gets up and chases me, only to bump into Sid. I laugh out loud. The two scowl at each other and then at me, unfairly blaming me for the collision, and go their separate ways.

At times I wonder, is the girl more obsessed than immature, or is it the other way round? What is she driving at? Is she comparing herself with Manasi? I haven't known a soul till date who has had any complaint against that graceful sweetheart. But I have to keep my involvement low, indulging her no further than those remarks she is allowed to pass in my presence to vent her frustrations.

Shekhar has been avoiding me since I spilled my plans of writing his biography. He finds me loitering around the campus gathering information, and bonding with Vatsala, but he doesn't object to my presence. This in no way means an approval. Rather, it is his way of ignoring me, to let me know that he or his decision isn't affected by all my self-driven interests. These are not good signs.

My thoughts are interrupted as a hand comes from the side and wraps itself around my shoulders. 'I am sorry, bro.'

It is Sid. I smile.

'But, one question.' He speaks before I can open my mouth. 'Pray tell me, how do you manage to get along with the loud-mouthed princess of Manhattan?'

He laughs and runs away. I laugh too.

He wouldn't understand why I wouldn't ever steer away from Vatsala. There's a madness about her, albeit different from the rest and beyond the boundaries of virtue and vice. She is the madness of water. Spirited, energetic and unstable. Just that, she is yet to be contained.

Late in the night Vatsala walks back with me. We stride through the less crowded paths of Chelsea. She is unusually quiet.

'What's going on?' I ask finally.

She stops a few steps later and stands before me blocking the way. Abruptly, I stop too.

'Brian,' she hisses. 'Every day on my way back I run my mind through Manasi's composition. And every day I end up with the same conclusion. This story needs me. My aspiration to dance with Shekhar is waiting for me to get up and take charge. As much as they try to ignore my presence, the climax is incomplete without me.'

My eyes grow wide.

'Don't trouble them, Vatsala. The show is just two months away.'

'Wait and watch. It's now or never,' she says with devilish determination and walks away.

The next day when I reach the guest house, Vatsala storms out of the entrance and bumps into me. She looks different, wearing traditional Indian clothes. I am about to compliment her, but I freeze as I see her gasping and panting, absolutely breathless. My eyes narrow, smelling trouble, trying to gauge what must have happened, when I spot Manasi standing at the balcony and looking down at her. Immediately I can figure out the turn of events that must have taken place a while ago. I try to speak, but Vatsala dodges me and leaves. I look up again.

Manasi stares at me, her eyes still as ice.

34

The Reckless Demand

VATSALA PANDIT
Manhattan, 2016

Raj Shekhar Subramanian is neck deep between rehearsals when Manasi smiles at me from above his shoulders. He turns to find who she is smiling at, and his eyes meet mine. He has seen me following the rehearsals very minutely. He seems happy that I have kept myself engaged. To a large extent, he is probably relieved that my attention now has other things to focus upon.

This morning I have taken some pains to look different. Instead of the usual track pants or loose pajamas and t-shirts that hug my skin, I have picked a soft green churidaar-kurta with the violet dupatta tied around my waist and left shoulder just like any other girl in Kala Mandir. Obviously, I look much better than all of them. His eyes rest on me for a few lovely moments before they are impatient again to get done. What I have to say is not as pleasant as the makeover. He instructs the others to carry on and slowly walks towards me, stopping at about an arm's length.

For a split second, I am scared to open my mouth. My throat dries up. I know this attention is temporary. The spell would break the moment I utter a word. Yet, I can't enjoy this for too long, lest the Dancer interpret my silence as my acquiescence to the defined role of observing, helping and learning from the rehearsals.

I come straight to the point. 'I want to perform in the inaugural show.'

He frowns. 'You think what we are doing is some kind of joke?'

'I have seen the length and breadth of your rehearsals, sir. Create a space for me. I'll take this several notches higher. Trust me.' A non-compromising urge is clear in my voice.

He is irritated again, but forces himself to calm down.

'It's too late, Vatsala. I wish we had something for you but at this point it won't be possible to make changes in the script and re-choreograph the minutes. I would request you to understand this. Please don't create a ruckus here. You will certainly be a part of the next show that Kala Mandir comes up with in New York.' He smiles reassuringly and carries on.

Does he really enjoy saying no to me every time? Or has he sworn not to learn with experience? About time he knew that I won't take 'no' for an answer. The word isn't meant for me.

I must make this happen. I will prove to him how my presence can bring about a huge difference in the act. But I must first convince someone to create a door for me through which I can enter. And I know who to approach.

With eyes set on my goal, I glance around to look for the only person who can help me. My ultimate target. Raj Shekhar

Subramanian's 'best' student! Today is when I have to take it head on.

To hell with all masks.

Unable to trace her anywhere, I stealthily leave the portico and dash into the elevator to reach Manasi's room.

35

The Confrontation

MANASI
Manhattan, 2016

I open the door to welcome Vatsala in, offering her lunch. She declines. She says she is here for a reason and doesn't intend to prolong her stay for unnecessary formalities. Taken off-guard by her sudden rudeness, I stand confused only to realize that this attack is because she wants to be a part of *Rasia*!

I understand this agony. It is a torture for a dancer to be competent, yet remain outcast when everyone else is on the job. But then, it is too late. I try to explain. But Vatsala isn't ready to listen.

She attacks me, her voice sharp, each word pointed like a spear.

'Didn't Mr Subramanian ever tell you that I am better than the best dancer in his team? I can perform such steps that no one here can even dare to think of. Matching with my speed is still a distant goal for all your so-called experts loitering around. I am a fortune to work with, lady.'

Immense frustration has broken down her sense of

boundaries. I try to say something to calm her down, but she stops me with an imperious gesture of her hand. 'When the audience finds me with Raj Shekhar Subramanian on stage, they would rave about the visual delight we are capable of creating simply by standing next to each other. Together we can weave a fantasy that every person watching it would love to touch and feel, and wish they were us.'

Vatsala seems to be on a journey to kill. She talks in a low voice so that her words don't reach outside the room. But these are the loudest I have heard in my entire life.

People don't speak to me like this. I have known myself to be soft, motherly, empathetic. None of these qualities have brought me any harshness in return. But this girl overflows with bitterness.

'I know it is difficult for the Dancer to accommodate me, because I am a potential threat to the most celebrated expertise of his wife. He thinks that you, Manasi, are his partner at every step of his existence. But the truth is something that he'll never acknowledge—up there on the stage, no one can complement him like I would.'

Footsteps outside make both of us turn towards the door. Vatsala rushes to lock it and looks back at me.

'Why do I feel, Manasi, that you and your husband are insecure? Why do I feel that both of you don't want me as a part of the inaugural show because it will naturally invite comparison between you and me?'

Vatsala's eyes glitter devilishly. She continues, unabashed and unapologetic, 'Subramanian's Indian strength collides with Chelsea's own beauty!' She grins dramatically. 'Such discussions would take their rounds, forcing you to face me and accept that I am a much better performer after only a few days of training by Raj Shekhar Subramanian, compared to the wife who has been trained all her married life.'

She comes closer to me, making me feel uncomfortable.

'The thought gives you tremors, doesn't it? Picked up from a dirty village in the remote east of India, you probably never thought of waking up one day to such riches and adulation, which comes to you not because you deserve it but simply because you are the wife of a veteran. You have cracked such a cheap deal, Manasi. All that you may have never ever thought of, was just a marriage away. You must have been destiny's child, or you are a shrewd strategist to make all this look like it was destined for you. You don't even look pretty, for one to believe you are capable of holding the attention of the god of Bharatanatyam for so many years. But convincingly you have trapped him into an image of perfection where he can't break away from his make-believe world of marital bliss. So, deserving ones like me won't ever have a chance! And if I bring this up, then I'll be humiliated so that I keep my mouth shut.'

Her eyes. Her voice. The vein on the side of her neck that bulges in rage. The sharp words which seem to slide so effortlessly off her tongue. Her resentment. Her anger. The acidic remarks. The cruelty.

For how long has she been nurturing all these? And against me? These were behind the cordial smiles I received during the last few days? I feel aghast. I don't know how to react.

'Are you in love with Shekhar, Vatsala?' The words slip from my mouth. In extreme shock, I have lost the power to hold back.

'Yes, I am,' she announces proudly without blinking an eye. 'I love Raj Shekhar Subramanian. I don't know whether this is right or wrong. But this is the truth.'

I let out a long sigh. Shekhar! My husband!

So she is behaving this crazy because Shekhar didn't pay heed to her reckless demands. What did she expect a respectable married man to do? Give in to her whims and cheat on his wife? She must have known right from the beginning that he won't be available to her. Or did she continue to harbour romantic expectations from Shekhar which he must have crushed ruthlessly?

Does love really make someone so bitter? She is trying her best to bruise me, hurt me, rip me apart; she wants me to bleed to death. And the girl says she is in love with the same person who has always filled me with a quest to live, explore, love and nurture?

This can't be love. Maybe infatuation, or mere obsession. The girl didn't understand Shekhar by any stretch of imagination. You have to give him space. Enormous space. So much that he finds himself lost in it; that is when he'll come looking for you.

You can't hold him captive to your expectations with smiles or tears. They are too complicated for him. He'll never come to you with flowers. But he has a unique place for everyone in his heart. In his own subtle ways, he lets everyone know how much he loves each of them.

Vatsala has probably tried to overstep her place, trying to take over what is mine. Shekhar must have resisted her vehemently. And that has made her feel insulted. I want to tell her that Shekhar did not humiliate her. Shekhar has neither the intention nor the time for these. It is she who is embarrassing herself. She is forcing herself to something that would pull her down to vast disgrace, putting to ruin her spirit and talents.

I remember Shekhar mentioning that she is a powerhouse performer. My mind throbs with anxiety.

She begins to speak again. I straighten to hear her. This time her voice is far more level.

'I can't stand and watch as mere audience, a show that can turn into a marvellous masterpiece with my participation, but remains compromised because a wife's possessiveness for her husband overshadows a performer's competence. If your dedication towards the art is true, if you have the courage to share the stage with me and let the audience judge who is better, then don't give me those stories. Create a place for me. Let's be fair to each other on the stage.'

She stops and gulps down water from the bottle she is carrying, her eyes fixed on mine.

'I'll prove to you that he is married to me,' she jolts me again, challenging the identity I have nurtured for seventeen years. 'But not with that silly vermillion in the partition of your hair. The stage is our wedlock. You are too shallow to understand this. So don't even try.' She looks away.

Vatsala has no idea what she has said, explaining all the achievements of my life as a huge shell of borrowed glory. My insides churn. This is more than personal. It is about Raj Shekhar Subramanian's public persona and all the factors that define his image. Vatsala wants me to separate my personal and professional relationship with Bharatanatyam and also with Shekhar, and return home to the husband but leave the stage to those who she believes deserve the spotlight better. She wants me to accept that the stage, which has now become a part of my breath, is just a forced extension of my personal life. She feels I have exploited my perks a bit too much.

Wait!

Doesn't this itself make for an excellent progression for *Rasia*? The battle of ownership between the incarnation who owns home and the one who shares work? Maybe, Parvati or Gauri and Kali!

For some time I remain quiet, visibly distracted, looking out of the window to arrange my thoughts and myself. My brain feels like a restless mess.

No, this can't be true, I decide. In Shekhar's life, I am his home and I am his work. There's no third person. This isn't just my hopeless possessiveness. I have known this man for too long now. My being is merged with his persona to an extent that I can't separate myself from him, even if I wish to.

But I must confirm this for my own good. I look at her again.

'What brings you to me? Had you convinced Shekhar, he would change things easily and reshuffle the existing course of the act. He has made last moment changes in the past. No one in Kala Mandir has questioned, let alone objected to his stance.'

Vatsala grows pale. She shifts her gaze. Slowly she shakes her head.

'I couldn't convince him, Manasi. And if I insist, he'll stubbornly defy logic. He will decide never to get convinced. It's more important for him to say "no" to me, rather than find sense in whatever I may have to offer.' She looks defeated.

I can't believe what I am hearing. She is trying to use me to convince Shekhar. The madness of this morning is a gamble to force some modifications to *Rasia*, by slaying the faith in my heart. The plan is, if she calls me insecure, then I will have to prove that I am not; else I just accept it and keep her away from *Rasia*.

I lift my eyes to look back at her.

Very well, then. I will create a role for Vatsala at the core of our story, which will give her the platform she's been waiting for. She would have a crucial performance with Shekhar to exhibit the dedication of her soul. She'll get to challenge me with her livid best on stage. This time her attacks won't be behind closed doors. Together we would perform a duet. Let the audience decide the fate of our respective holds on the art. And of course, Shekhar.

I will not do this to prove anything. I am not fighting to protect my rights either. I am simply making way for Vatsala to fight for herself, if she really believes that there is something spectacular she has on offer. And yes, I will convince Shekhar too.

I sit engrossed and sleepless late into the night, my existence illuminated within the screen of my laptop.

> Shiva and Kali's lasya-tandava ends with strong sounds of the drum. All other forms of music or chants are silenced when the drum plays in mono-beats just like the ticking of a watch. Kali stands there astounded while Shiva takes slow steps backwards. A spotlight focusses to the top of the stairs, where Gauri stands gracefully, wrapped in a costume of white with an elaborate red border. Soon the drums are replaced by the conch once

again, to signal the rebirth that Gauri symbolizes.

Gauri is another incarnation of Parvati, and is considered to be Shiva's perfect wife. She is known as the fertility goddess, the motherly form of Shakti. While Kali is the black Goddess, the name 'Gauri' comes from her fair complexion.

Shiva must go back to Gauri!

He slowly moves away from Kali, walking towards the stairs. Kali stops Shiva to remind him that she, not anyone else, is his true consort. She is the executor of his vision who carries his philosophies to their fulfilment. Shiva doesn't stop. Enraged, Kali calls upon Gauri to legitimately claim Shiva and take him away if she can. Gauri comes forward on the raised platform, each movement of hers soaked in calm confidence and pride for being the queen of the Lord's heart. Kali and Gauri performs a jugalbandi* challenging each other at every step to establish their respective rights over Shiva.

Gauri invites Shiva back home, where wife, children, grains, prosperity, opulence and indulgence await him. Kali, in contrast, tries to hold him back to the cremation ground, where death is the greatest leveller; where the soul attains freedom in permanence; where only the truth stands, devoid of pretence. She promises nothing but herself to the Lord.

After the duet, both Kali and Gauri bow before Shiva and wait for his decision. Shiva maintains that he

---

*Jugalbandi: duet

must go back to Gauri, because that is the inevitable binding of destiny.

Kali offers to give up her individual existence and merge with him as one so she can stay with and within the Lord forever. Amidst the sounds of strong winds prophesying a storm, the fire of the torches swaying violently and the bells hanging from above swinging to and fro with ruthless aggression, Kali walks ahead and stands in front of Shiva. Lights fade allowing her to disappear.

36

The Reunion

RAJ SHEKHAR SUBRAMANIAN
Manhattan, 2016

I have noticed Manasi's sudden quiet in the last few days. She looks viciously obsessed when she is between rehearsals, but distracted otherwise. Since both of us have been spending almost sleepless nights, I hardly find time for her. Manasi grows silent when there's a storm inside. Her usual cheerfulness then goes for a toss. She remains preoccupied within her own restlessness.

Is it the stress of show? Or something else?

She was completely drowned into things when the troupe arrived at New York. She was bubbling with energy, eager to tell me and know from me everything about the last few months. In between rehearsals whenever our eyes locked, she smiled divinely. For a while I remained lost in that, before plunging back into the chores. I don't know when Manasi has stepped into this overshadowing silence. I have seen her staring blankly at something, completely disconnected from the world surrounding her.

Our sleep schedules are erratic these days. The troupe works and rehearses most of the time. Whenever the tasks set for the day seem to be more or less complete, whatever be the hour, they try to catch up with some rest. In between such strenuous schedules, this evening I find Manasi walking up to the room around eleven in the night. Quickly, I end my day with a few instructions here and there and follow her upstairs. She is unbraiding and untangling her hair when the sound of the door closing behind makes her turn. Soft emotions play across her face. With every step I take to bridge the distance between us, I can see her transforming into a light feather, the ground slipping away from beneath our feet like sands under the pressure of a sudden wave.

She knows I have come for her.

Our eyes are locked into each other's as if nothing else exists. Life reanimates her tired bones; she sits up slowly. Her bare shoulder titillates me; she makes no attempt to pull up her sleeves. Her loose hair arouses raw desire that had been sleeping inside me for months. Whatever energy I may have spent rehearsing all through the day seems to be replenished in multiples, as this woman blushes like we are going to make love for the first time.

In the next abrupt moment though, she looks resigned. Strangely she tries to focus back into her hair.

I frown. What is she trying to hide?

I walk up to stand very close to her. I touch her with a hand on her back. With the other, I lift her face towards mine. Manasi tries to look away. I bring her back to me. She hangs her face down and touches my chin with her forehead.

There's no hurry to make her speak. I run my hands over

her skin and caress the back of her neck. Manasi pulls herself closer to me so that no part of her body remains deprived of the touch that seems to tame her restless soul. Months of restraint engulfs us as an engrossing passion to own each other with inexplicable urgency. Slowly, I pull her to bed. In the dark I can feel her internal agitation.

Just when I am preparing to ask, Manasi speaks.

'I have done something you won't like.'

I frown. Everything about *Rasia* is Manasi's; why then does she need to say this? I have interfered as little as possible. The composition has moved exactly the way she wanted. What more is it that she could have done, which happened without my knowledge? I look down at her, waiting.

Tension grips her body. 'I have asked Vatsala to play Gauri.'

With a jerk I sit up, leaving her on the bed. Manasi springs up behind me. She tries to read my expression, in the darkness of the hour. The silence between us feels like the still of the dead. With each solitary music of night, Manasi grows increasingly anxious. She runs her fingers over my muscles, tight with displeasure. My mind races to understand what could have prompted her to do this. Manasi touches me from behind and supports herself on my bare back.

'How long would you keep her away from the stage, Shekhar? She deserves to be with us. You know it. Let's just be fair to her talents?' she says softly, with half-hearted confidence.

The prolonged silence feels unbearable. But I wait, trying to comprehend this strange development. Manasi pulls herself in front of me and touches the side of my neck. For a while we look at each other. Manasi's large eyes carry the yearning of a woman waiting for her man. They also reflect her inner turmoil for asking something that I would not be happy about. She is disturbed, as much as I am offended. I calm down, as the urge in Manasi's eyes tear through my restraints. I let my hand girdle her waist and look back at her, trying to read whatever is still left for me to know.

'So you extended *Rasia* and introduced Gauri just to accommodate Vatsala?' I ask.

Manasi doesn't answer that.

'Let me do this Shekhar, please. It's important for me to let the truth unfold.' She loses her focus. Unmindfully, she sits with me, her attention wandering.

This isn't the Manasi I have known. My wife is radiant when I am around. She talks endlessly, smiles, plays pranks, seduces; she tries to stop me from thinking anything beyond her. The time I spend with her, she gathers every bit of it for herself.

Where is she treading today, leaving me alone even as we lie on the same bed?

I touch her cheek and turn her face back towards me.

'Let her satisfy herself, Shekhar. If you stop her today, all her life she'll feel that she could have altered her destiny if circumstances were in her favour.'

My eyes narrow. Vatsala has bypassed my word and spoken to Manasi. I can gather Manasi is deeply hurt.

'I did not extend *Rasia* just because Vatsala demanded so,' she says. 'I was not too satisfied with the end of the composition. Look at the script now, Shekhar. Gauri is the perfect end to our concept!'

She tries to smile.

I wait for a while, watching the smile spread hesitantly on to her lips. 'Where did *Rasia* come from?' I ask.

The smile disappears.

'I don't know!' Manasi fumbles. 'There isn't a fixed time when this had started taking shape, Shekhar. Maybe it was somewhere deep inside me, embedded since childhood. Or maybe it is just an expression that came to my mind while participating with you in endless performances. There was no concrete story with me, but an idea may have originated in the subconscious. It grew as I did, under your guidance.'

I lower her back on to the bed. 'Why didn't you ever tell me, Manasi?'

Manasi looks confused, her natural innocence coming through. 'What could I tell you? At times, I would visualize us creating and performing this tale, in bits and pieces, but I wasn't sure what exactly this was all about and how it can be used as a backbone for creating a script. But when you suddenly asked me to design a concept and take it forward for the inaugural show, this was the only idea I had partially ready with me.'

She moans as I am already exploring her. Her body shivers. Before we lose ourselves to each other in the pleasure that is as deep as the soul, my voice, soaked in masculine desires, whispers in her ears.

'I want to write the conclusion of *Rasia*.'

Manasi is not in control of herself to answer this; neither does it require an answer.

I am wide awake when the clock strikes two. Manasi lies beside me, deep in sleep. Her anxious mind seems to have relaxed finally. But my insomniac nerves are still active. I remember

Nobarun Bhattacharya's voice advising me during difficult times, 'When all doors close for you, you come back to yourself, submit and seek submission. That is when you are close to God.'

Today I face no deadlock. But peace certainly lies in submission. The conclusion of *Rasia* would mark my submission.

Quickly I lift myself from the bed, switch on the reading lamp on the table and open my laptop to put it down in words—'Shiva's Confession'. Shiva would address this to Gauri, inviting her to sing with him in appreciation of the black Goddess.

SHIVA'S CONFESSION:

As Kali merges with me, O Gauri, my soul shivers with the wisdom and power of Adi Shakti, flowing as blood through my veins. Each part of my body feels dedicated to the sole purpose which I and Kali stand for jointly. I owe her my inseparability and indispensability. I am vowed to fulfil her innate longings. As she resides within me, her influence would reflect upon my passion and dedication, as much as your youth and abundance, O Gauri, reflects in my pleasure and vastness.

Kali, the most misunderstood Goddess, would remain bound to me with a pledge of unconditionality. Mortals have never worshipped her as my beloved. The Devas have kept a distance from her lest she challenges their pride. Even I may have undervalued her diligence and commitment in support of the cause I represent. With all my forces gathered together, I invite mortals and immortals to perceive Kali within their attempts to give up on the false existence that is disconnected from their real self. I shall inhabit cremation grounds to find Kali, whenever I am wrapped in your Maya of worldly pleasures, O Gauri. Together we will grant liberation of the illusory ego and destroy attachment of individuals to their temporary bodies.

Kali, my consort, is as pure as the Ganga that flows from my head, as furious as the fangs of the snake hanging around my neck, as grounded as the ashes on my body, and as indifferent as the mind that causes my detachment. Kali and I are one, and we are equal; she resides within me as power and truth and is the strength of my being. She is present within the children I am a father to, the flow of time I represent; the destruction I create is she; my damru is hers as much as it is mine; she would be as constant and varied as the moon of the night sky adorning my hair; without her I am vigourless, lifeless matter who remains fallen on the earth, weak and unable to perform my duties. Join me, O Gauri, to celebrate the selflessness of Kali and solemnly acknowledge her contributions in balancing the cosmos!

At the end of Shiva's confession, Gauri and Shiva shall perform a Kalika Stotra and mark the end of *Rasia*.

37

Call of the Stage

VATSALA PANDIT
Manhattan, 2016

Finally, it is time for the stage!

The ever-buzzing guest house is as silent as death. In Kala Mandir no one works on the day of the show. No rehearsals, no preparations, no last-minute strategizing, no panic, no stress. Everything is finalized one day before. Everyone relaxes the way they want. Most of the boys are watching soccer on television. Shekhar and his wife have gone out for a long walk; my eyes are fixed at the gate awaiting their return. Some known and half-known faces greet us with their good wishes for the evening.

I sit chit-chatting with Natarajan, Varanya and Ali. Being senior dancers, both Varanya and Ali are moulded as per the standards of their high-headed chief. They behave like his clones. They are bemused and intrigued by my last-minute entry, but never ask a word. The troupe has been extremely cooperative. Their warmth helps me survive those merciless eyes that display no interest towards me, yet seem to know everything.

Manasi, though, shows no contempt. She is as supportive

as the rest of the gang. It's me who feels feverish every time she is around. I try to engage with the rehearsals as if nothing else exists on the planet. Otherwise, I just hide somewhere to avoid her. But Manasi doesn't seem to carry the remnants of that fretful morning. She smiles at everyone, even me.

Varanya leisurely munches on her breakfast.

'Remember those early days at Kala Mandir?' She smiles. 'At the end of the planning and rehearsals we played cards or chess. Akka did not know either; we taught her both. She remained very bad with chess till she gave it up after a while.'

'Akka gave it up? We banned her off the chess board,' Ali laughs. 'She always had the most miserable moves. When she knew she would inevitably lose, she jumbled up the contents on the board and ran away.'

Varanya smiles too. 'But Anna never lost in chess. He and everyone else though, lost frequently when Akka would spread the cards. She somehow managed to manipulate the cards with some strange turn of hands. Anna grew livid that his wife has cheated, but this was one space where Akka never took him seriously.'

Ali picks up a sandwich from Varanya's plate. 'She always said—I am not playing to win; I am just having fun. And she laughed every time Anna lost. She argued that she never manipulated the cards; it was all about the magic of her hands.'

Varanya looks at me. 'In those days, a few people who never knew each other before, came together with just a belief that one day they'll make it big. And that belief had only one face—Raj Shekhar Subramanian.'

Greedily I devour all these stories. They introduce to me

some other person with the same name, who is loving, innocent, adorable, complaining, accepting; perhaps more humane.

Natarajan cuts through my momentary distractions. 'Everyone remotely close to Anna knows that he always has a list with him in which he has written down everything he wants to achieve with a deadline specified for each item on the list. He never shows that to anyone, not even Akka. But he achieves everything on it nevertheless. This New York chapter of Kala Mandir was certainly not on that list. He had aimed it for a later date, that too not with much certainty. I can't really believe all this is happening so soon.'

Just when I begin to feel proud, Varanya kills my mood, 'It is only because of Akka! She has stood by him like a rock.'

I flare up. Everyone here seems to worship the goddess of sacrifice! I stop myself sooner than what my temperament is known for. Not now. Not here. Let's meet on the stage!

Manasi certainly is a brave woman. She hasn't been unfair in scripting my role. Rather she has given me the scope to prove myself. There is a duet with Manasi and then a Kalika Stuti which I'll perform with Shekhar. During rehearsals, everyone applauded my proficiency. Although Manasi is the main choreographer for *Rasia*, I have mysteriously been granted a lot of liberty with my steps.

I have been a ballet dancer before, but never have I experienced this kind of togetherness. The team I danced with in the club was very professional. Perfection was a non-negotiable holy word. It is the same here, but interpersonal relations at Kala Mandir are far more profound. People here have grown up with each other. They have complete access to each other's personal lives. Everyone is a part of this troupe not only because they worship the stage; these people can give up their lives for their mentors.

I get up from the floor walking leisurely to the water tank to quench my thirst. When I finish, I turn and bump into Ali. He looks at me strangely.

Uncomfortable with his stare, I ask, 'What?'

Ali rests his back on the adjoining wall.

'Anna always says, dance like there is nothing beyond this performance. After every show of Kala Mandir, we are all dead. That's what we have been taught to do. That is our philosophy. Every new act is a resurrection; we are reborn then. With the end of every act we are expected to leave behind the vanity we may have acquired when the audience cheers for us. We start afresh from scratch. Everyone here follows this verdict as per our own human capacities. When one of us tends to indulge in the celebrations for too long, Anna snaps them out of it.'

I go pale, as he rips apart my obstinate confidence. Along with it goes the open secret which no one here had dared to touch upon so far. Affectionately, he places a hand on my head.

'We have not yet performed, but you have already reached the stage that would supposedly start at the end of the show. You might be walking a dangerous path, girl. We aren't permitted to do this.'

He gets going, and halts again. 'Till the time someone stops you here, trying to correct you, you know you are with us. But when no one stops you, you have no idea how severe that pain of rejection is.'

Ali walks away with a smile that speaks much beyond what

he has told me, leaving me stranded and isolated, unsure of where I should be headed.

∽

The auditorium is packed by 5 in the evening. All the tickets are sold out. The important dignitaries have taken their places. The media is ready to shoot. Every performer waits in the green room, holding their breath. The bell rings at 5.30 p.m., sharp. The compere shares a brief history of Kala Mandir.

And then, the loud beats of the drum…

This is the cue for Emraan. Swiftly he hugs Shekhar as tightly as he can, and leaves for the stage with long strides. With the conch shell held against his mouth, Emraan appears on top of the stairs as Lord Krishna.

This is not the Lord who plays havoc with women's dreams and devotion; neither is this the mischievous child who steals butter from pots hung out of his reach. He is not the son, or brother, or friend; rather, he is the God of Gods who resides within each soul. This is Lord Krishna from the Gita, exploring his own tale of creation, sustenance and destruction. His body is straight and erect, with a fast progression of postures being exhibited with great finesse. The nervousness that caused Emraan to sweat inside the green room has transformed into vibrant energy. The audience is captive to Krishna's Monologue. As the evening progresses, Emraan dominates the act not only with his performance, but also dismisses the concomitant music with his ghungroos, activated to swift footwork creating his own solitary track soaked in passionate energy, prophesying the dark!

His part is meant to be a transformation from the subtle to the energetic. He concludes Krishna's Monologue invoking Kali, as he balances his entire body on the floor with one knee; the other leg stretched backwards with the knee bent in the middle and hands pulled forward into a namaskaram.

Next is Manasi. I look to my left.

38

Dance of Desire

RAJ SHEKHAR SUBRAMANIAN
Manhattan, 2016

She turns to look at me one last time before running out of the green room. I nod, and she is gone. I follow her till the curtains, to watch from the back the first independent composition of my wife.

With Krishna's exit, the stage turns dark. Soon a garland of hands created with the yellow light of the projector goes around the neck of a female body who stands at the same place that was occupied by Krishna a while back. It illuminates only those parts of her body where the hands fall and move in a circle, retaining the rest of the body in dark. The ornaments on her body and metallic weapons in her hand shine through the limited light. The figure looks mysterious and ethereal; and unnerving. Human skulls created with light float on the corner walls of the stage. There is the strong roar of stormy winds in the background. The bells and lanterns hanging above sway, threatening to fall any moment.

Tashi's Nirvaan has done a splendid job along with

Natarajan. Arjun and Dhriti too have brought heaven down on earth with the way they have set the stage.

Manasi's representation of Kali is ferocious and violent, soaked in a beauty that doesn't have language. Kali's fierce is such a contrast to Manasi's calm! The wildness in her eyes, the euphoria in her body, the commanding choreography is in complete contrast to the poise and patience that define her personality otherwise. The black Goddess has blessed her with miraculous power this evening, sharing generously with her an uncompromising, irresistible energy. Manasi sets the stage on fire with elaborate expressions and movements, which steal from the audience their right to blink.

Up there on stage, I can see a reflection of my own life.

Manasi is telling me things that words can't contain. A vision that remained dormant within her, voiceless and expressionless; something that Nobarun Bhattacharya kept exploring but couldn't reach to the depths of. Kali is a philosophy that governs her. As much as she is bound by the rules I have laid down, she remains invincible in her fathomless pursuit of liberation, where emotions like anger or pride have no place. Those insecurities and loneliness that I keep under wraps is untangling slowly. Perhaps this sync with Kali empowered Manasi to forgive Vatsala's impudence and yet respect her talent with a deserving appreciation. Something I couldn't do.

And *Rasia* is her deepest manifestation. Through the act her forceful creative voice comes through, like it has never done in the past.

As she moves across the stage with vigour, I can feel the shackles of my own pride loosening. My drive to exercise complete control and build everything by myself are mocking at me. By distributing work among different members of Kala Mandir, allowing them to bring forward their best talents, Manasi has simply proved that everyone has a unique aptitude to offer in a joint act; my rigidities are so obsolete. I made them over-dependent on me so they can never abandon me. Manasi tells me, give them wings to fly and they will immortalize our names on the horizon they occupy.

All through these years I have preached that personal pride and resultant arrogance should never be encouraged. I never realized that I too have been a victim to the vices I opposed.

The orphan who started his life within the broken walls of a shabby building has always overpowered my existence and I have willingly fallen prey to it. The domination that never allowed anyone to experiment with personal creative goals is now lying shattered, like shards of glass all across the stage. Manasi's exuberant footwork is scattering them far and wide, forever beyond my reach.

Sounds of the damru! This is my entry.

Swiftly I move to take position in the darkness of the stage, allowing the blue lights to illuminate me subsequently. Sid and Sandy have given me a white costume with heavy embroideries of animal skin and thin zari work in the border. They wanted Shiva's costume to have some sort of conjunction with Gauri's, representing their togetherness in body and being. I have also been given a long rudraksh garland to be placed across my shoulders and waist so that it fits on the body diagonally. A trident has been painted elaborately across my back. Unlike the

U-shaped teeka* made with sandalwood on Krishna, I have three white lines horizontally placed across my forehead which is cut across by a straight line made of red kumkum.

Just before I enter the stage, I bend to touch the ground with my head. Today I'll perform not for the world, but for the woman who united my conscious with my subconscious. I will put to test every bit of Bharatanatyam I am blessed with and challenge my own expertise, to serve this woman who has served me all her life.

I don't know whether there is another way to give. But this evening, there is nothing more important than the next few hours, that I can give Manasi. This has to be our moment of truth.

The Lasya-Tandava that follows exhibits some of the most aesthetic moves. The more Shiva indulges in rugged pleasure, the greater speed Kali seems to gather in her spirit. With each and every beat of music, we provoke each other to embrace the divine. Both of us are caught up in a very personal journey exploring, deconstructing and reconstructing ourselves through the well-rehearsed act. As our conjugal performance comes to an end, both me and Manasi can feel the extent to which we have stretched ourselves this evening, way deeper than all rehearsals and choreographic predictions. Our bodies ache, but our souls feel buoyant. This is our very private language of communicating with each other. The audience today is a secondary enthusiast, far disconnected from the exchange that is happening on the stage.

Music halts abruptly at the climax. Shiva detaches himself

---

*A holy mark worn on the forehead by Hindus

from the bonds of Kali and declares, he must go back to Gauri. The top of the stairs are illuminated once again. Vatsala stands there awaiting her part.

Manasi once again owns the evening with her desperate call to the disconnected Shiva, longing for him to remain with her, to accept her, and to recognize her as his true consort. Her pleas merge with her pain, as the Lord stands apart because it is the call of the cosmos that he returns to Gauri.

Unable to dissuade Shiva, the enraged Kali invites Gauri to separate Shiva from her if she can.

39

Rasia

BRIAN HERRETT
Manhattan, 2016

The viewers occupy their seats in deep exhilaration, intoxicated and enthralled by whatever their eyes see, ears hear, senses feel and brains absorb.

When Manasi and Shekhar are creating magic before the audience, time stands still. They are known to bring magnificent creativity to the fore every time they are on the stage, but this is something more than that. No rehearsals, no arrangements, no pre-decided gimmicks can guarantee the spontaneous vigour that seems to possess them. They are probably giving each other the best performance of their lives. The whole of Kala Mandir watches spellbound. No one utters a word. This is surreal.

Vatsala stands in a corner, watching in dismay the splendour that unfolds before her.

Manasi is no longer the soft-spoken, intimidated, docile woman that she usually comes across as. Her exhilaration is unmistakeable and unstoppable. In Vatsala's eyes, open wide in awe, I can see perceptions changing.

The audience is actually watching Kali, telling them the story of an extraordinary woman. When Shekhar joins her, she meets a partner transcending lives. Their togetherness is not just the tale of two people uniting for a purpose; their thoughts, actions and discipline are bound into each other with some holy connection. In the Dance of Desire, Shekhar and Manasi weave the tale of their own indispensability towards each other on stage, as much as they explain the dependence of Shiva on Kali.

I walk ahead to stand with Vatsala in the isolated corner where a passage from the auditorium connects with the green room.

When she was chosen for the act of Gauri, she had taken some preparatory measures.

'Understand Gauri well enough before representing her. Read up everything available on Gauri Mata;* Varanya will help you grasp the details about the deity,' Manasi had told her.

Vatsala had also dug out information from the internet and repeatedly watched the dance compositions of various forms that were based on the Goddess. After understanding her character in sufficient detail, she started with some calming exercises combining yoga and meditation that Manasi had shown her.

'My presence on the stage won't be more than forty-five minutes, but I want to approach those forty-five minutes with the sincerity of a protagonist. See how the rest of the gang become mere accessories supporting me there,' she had told me. 'So what if I am a last-minute entry to the act. True, the role has been carved out only to accommodate my request that

---

*Mata: mother goddess

morning...' She stopped abruptly.

'Request!' I had laughed. Sadly, she looked at me, unprepared for the unexpected sarcasm from her only friend. But I was offended. 'You had attacked Manasi—attacked the very core of her being and fibre of her life for the last seventeen years. You sought to destroy her peace and fill her with despondency,' I told her.

Meekly she accepted it, but there was no way she could correct anything about it. 'I never really expected Manasi to make such prominent modifications to accommodate me in the show,' she confessed.

'What were you trying to do, Vatsala?' I had asked furiously. 'Did you expect Manasi to be intimidated by you?'

'No!' I could see her arrogance returning. 'I just said the things I did to shake up her emotions. I thought that would work negatively on her conviction.'

I had laughed again. 'Do you have any idea who you are dealing with? You have underestimated the strength of this woman, poor girl. In return for all your nastiness, Manasi has opened her arms and welcomed you. You thought you can destroy her confidence; her place in the world? Her world is not as shallow as yours. During the rehearsals, none of us opened our mouths. But everyone knew what you are foolishly trading. I feel pity for you!'

The girl was not accustomed to hear this language from me. She sank with each word I spoke. With barely concealed anxiety, her eyes bore into mine, questioning hopelessly whether I too would abandon her in the hours ahead.

Vatsala probably would have enjoyed this game, had Manasi

resisted her attempts and pushed her aside to a corner, never to look at her again. She then would have fought back with a vengeance. By paving her path to the game she constructed herself, yet remaining passive by refusing to participate in anything vulgar, Manasi had filled her with embarrassment and guilt.

In her own soft way, she had invited Vatsala to take away Shekhar if she could, just like Kali did to Gauri in her composition, *Rasia*!

God knows whether to pacify me or reassure herself, Vatsala had said stubbornly, 'After *Rasia*, Raj Shekhar Subramanian will speak another language. Just like I ensured that he came to me all the way from India, similarly I will chain him to me with a performance he'll not be able to ignore, as much as he'd like to.'

I had picked up my bag and left; she called from behind but I didn't stop.

From an isolated corner of the passage, Vatsala has been watching Shekhar and Manasi set the benchmark of the evening to an inhuman level. With the progress of every beat, with every minute that permanently leaves behind the other, Vatsala experiences within her a growing restlessness to hit the stage. I can sense that turbulence as I stand behind her. She turns to take my hand into hers, happy that our argument a few evenings ago had not ruined our friendship. I am the only one to wish her well before her performance begins.

Finally, the moment arrives.

Vatsala assumes position in the darkness. Lights focus on her.

When Kali calls Gauri to come and win Shiva back, Gauri stands undeterred. With a hand raised to bless the world with her Godly affection, she bends the upper half of her body to look at Kali. Soon both of them initiate the most awaited duet. Gauri performs on the raised platform above the stairs; Kali does her act on the ground of the stage. The two women coordinate beautifully, no one crosses their respective spheres.

Vatsala is flawless; Manasi sublime. Kali wishes to claim her rights; Gauri is driven to protect her Dharma.* Kali is deprived of what Gauri has in abundance. Kali is passion personified; Gauri exudes beauty and grace. Kali is the cause that Shiva represents; Gauri is the effect. The glory of being the Lord's supreme queen is locked within the expressions of Gauri. When Manasi's ghungroos brought alive by her ardent footwork makes the audience wake up to the womanly longings of Kali, the cheerful Vatsala's heavenly postures soak them in her inherent happiness. And the contrast that both of them create in the process is breathtaking.

After the jugalbandi, when Shiva still wants to return to Gauri, Kali offers to surrender to her Lord. She takes slow steps to come and stand before Shiva, defeated but not dishonoured! The lights go off.

As Kali symbolically merges into Shiva, his body language undergoes a fierce transformation from majestic to exuberant. The auditorium is frozen, watching Shekhar shake his body stretching his hands outward, opening himself for Shakti to reside within his body and manifest as a part of him. With unpredictable movements conceived in tender intimacy and robust devotion, he delightfully expresses the possession of power

---

*Dharma: Indian philosophy. The eternal law of the cosmos, inherent in the very nature of things

and wisdom that should alight with the unison of Shiva and Kali. Multiple lights of different colours are thrown at him. Conch shells play till eternity.

Shiva invites Gauri to join him in Kalika Stotram.

This is the moment. All music is turned off. In a free voice, undiluted by any accompanying music, Sulochana starts singing. Shekhar and Vatsala are no longer a man and woman expressing their rights and desires. They are now devotees of Mahakali. With chaste movements, they describe the form and appearance of the black Goddess, and her contributions to retain the balance in the cosmos. Their movements have feminine compassion merged with male vigour, which both Shekhar and Vatsala portray with remarkable balance. Together they look like the most enigmatic pair, understanding and supporting each other, communicating majestic knowledge immersed in the depth of their faith.

Amidst pin-drop silence the show comes to an end. When the curtains fall no one says a word. No one moves or makes the slightest noise. A deathly silence continues for a while till the audience comes out of their spell and cheer in unison. Applause echoes all over the auditorium as every single soul rises from their seats extending a warm welcome to Kala Mandir's New York chapter.

I rush behind the curtains. The entire group has come up hugging and greeting each other. Everyone runs to Shekhar. He is now somewhere there, lost in the crowd. Everyone congratulates each other and exclaims that the job is finally done well.

Vatsala stands aside, watching them cheer. Other than a few scattered handshakes, no one is interested in her. Not that anyone has cast her out either. Stealthily she turns and leaves.

For one last time, she looks back at the stage, then walks away briskly with her head down.

I watch her go. This would be a difficult evening for the girl. I wait for a while, and march ahead looking for Shekhar.

I look for him all through the auditorium and green rooms and halls, which are now flooded with delegates, viewers and the media. But Shekhar is nowhere. With her usual smiling demeanour, Manasi moves through the crowd, attending to everyone.

Finally, I find him, standing alone on the vacant corridor at the far end, supporting his back against a pillar and looking at the sky.

And in the next few minutes I have the contract of the biography in my hands, signed by Shekhar. The Dancer excuses himself, leaving me shocked and happy at the same time. I check the signature on the papers once again and look up to find Shekhar disappearing through the connecting corridors to the rear end of the building, where he would have no one to face.

I know where he is headed.

40

The Introspection

VATSALA PANDIT
Manhattan, 2016

As I walk up the stage this evening, something changes. Competing with Manasi or compelling Raj Shekhar Subramanian isn't so important anymore. Those seem much lesser goals, compared to the beats I feel within my soul. A sense of responsibility is taking over.

I am the concluding part of the act. I can't compromise with the standard of the show, which the mentors have built up over the last two hours. I have to be at par. I have to give the show its deserving end.

Probably this is what Ali had tried to explain a few evenings ago.

'Bharatanatyam will even you out; you will flow with the collective emotion. Nothing will remain yours ever again,' he had said.

Finally, when the stage is mine, I want the world to know that nothing more beautiful has ever occurred to me before, nor would something more beautiful ever come to this stage.

This is the moment that encapsulates it all. I want to tell the world that Bharatanatyam has just met one of its most ardent representations.

As I match steps with Shekhar, the blood in my veins pumps with a boisterous thrill. In front of the whole world I stand by him, touch him, emote with him and declare myself his. The fulfilment of this long cherished dream fills me with blissful energy as my body grows more ecstatic with every passing moment. Here I am, Shiva's principal consort to whom the God must return at the end of the day; beyond that I am Raj Shekhar Subramanian's partner, whom he would remember for life every time he looks back at this journey.

These are the last few minutes that I would stay connected with the Dancer. Even if he wishes to, he can't throw me aside. I give myself to those moments, writing my name in eternity. I express myself with a language that comes from my innermost longing, casting off every doubt of being disowned once again as soon as the curtains go down.

I open myself to this show agreeing to be dead by the end.

Standing beside Shekhar, I allow myself the full pleasure of a perfect synchronicity. Satisfaction sweeps through my chest as we extend our hands into a prolonged namaskaram.

Curtains drop.

It takes me a few seconds to come to terms with the present.

It's over.

Shekhar has already moved on. He is being hugged and congratulated. I refuse to merge with his stream of followers. I stand apart, still not done with the time I spent with him on stage. Our choreographic togetherness was unscathed by the disharmony he maintains with me otherwise. I can't let that feeling of intimacy dissolve in the common emotions of the crowd. I hold them very close to my memories and walk out stealthily, to guard myself from being discovered as running away with a little bit of Raj Shekhar Subramanian.

All of us have probably gone through our own personal journeys, more than merely putting up an act. The journey doesn't address the complications of the path, but the destination is as clear as a rain-washed morning. Thunders are left behind. Only a polish of the clean persists.

Manasi shares a spiritual bond with the Dancer. She has a strange command over his brain in a way they themselves don't realize. Most of his emotions and their visual interpretations get filtered through her with a distinct, unfailing decorum. He responds, guarding her interests and glory. The Dancer may not have known this about himself.

The bridge that separates me from Raj Shekhar Subramanian is Manasi. However much I walk towards him, I never reach him. Rather, since I have already tried, I know that the distance only multiplies with every step I take. Manasi won't stop me from walking. She'll just stretch herself far and wide, nullifying my capacities.

A feeble tear trickles down my face; I wipe it away.

I stand in the green room, facing the huge mirror. I look beautiful. My hands, body and face actually look like those of a heavenly being. The woman who had travelled this long way with an obsessive wish to steal Raj Shekhar Subramanian away from the world, the woman who attacked Manasi with verbal malice like a devil, the woman who left the green room a few hours ago to put up an ambitious performance, and the woman who stands before the mirror now, seem to be four different characters! The first was a child; the second had just woken up to a very potent desire of adolescence; the third was living the resounding dream of a lifetime; and the fourth facing a deep truth that her brightest desire manifested few horizons away, in someone else's life.

I don't realize when tears have started washing my face. Resigned, I place myself on the adjoining chair, hastily trying to get out of the elaborate hairdo and costumes. I want to run away to a safe haven, disconnected from everything here, and bury my face into my pillow. I want to sleep.

Distracted and unmindful, I rapidly undo the jewellery, when there is a knock on the door.

Who the hell could have remembered me at this hour?

I turn to look at the door. My limbs lack the strength to move. A knock again and the door opens by itself. Shekhar walks in.

Startled and conscious almost immediately, I spin the chair and stand up.

He looks tired and calm, but the sparkle in his eyes is there as always. He stands just a few metres away; yet he is so distanced that even if I touch him, he won't be touched. I am not sure how I should react to this person who comes in voluntarily today to stand alone in this room with me.

Mind unsteady and body frozen, I wait to hear the cruel words he must have carried for me this evening.

41

Shiva's Confession

RAJ SHEKHAR SUBRAMANIAN
Manhattan, 2016

This evening she chooses to remain alone, instead of basking in the adulation outside. Probably she wouldn't have opened the door had I not pushed it from outside. She looks at me with a resignation which has taken away more than her usual aggression.

It happens, when you perish and take yourself back to the line from where it all began. Success too is a kind of death; you have to be born again to chase the next. I can see that in Vatsala today, in her lack of interest towards anything that connects to this place. She looks much more grown-up than what she was only a day back.

'You were very good this evening, Vatsala,' I tell her. 'Your act added such value to the show, just as every beautiful journey should have a well-deserved end. Without you, *Rasia* would feel so abrupt and incomplete. Though I wasn't in favour of you participating so early, I am happy that you did and lifted the spirits of the performance with your natural charm.'

She doesn't seem convinced with my compliments. She just

smiles faintly, then looks away.

'Let go of me, Vatsala,' I utter.

Vatsala looks up once again, confused.

'Stop holding me back; let go of me,' I say again. 'It is not just Bharatanatyam that you find in me; your interest goes deeper. It feels like a forbidden presence to have you around. There is nothing that I can ever give you, Vatsala. Nothing in return for the evening made beautiful by your exquisite moves; nothing in return for the satisfaction I achieved while training you; nothing for those childish emotions you have nurtured for me in your heart. There may have been nothing wrong with you wanting me. It is just that I don't belong to you. And there is nothing that I can do tonight, to put your distressed mind at rest.'

I stop, searching for words. Vatsala stares at me in dismay.

'I know this is not an honourable response to a gift as pure as love. You may have felt that my non-response towards you was undeserved. But the truth is, I never owned or disowned you. You did. So, I'm afraid, you will have to solemnly disown whatever you have owned unfairly, knowing from the depth that this is not to be. That, I understand, is a very difficult process. I tried to stop you from entering it but you didn't pay heed.'

Vatsala's expression is completely blank. Perhaps she has never seen me speaking with affection and tenderness, explaining myself instead of commanding. Her eyes fill with tears.

'Vatsala, please don't feel that I can't be yours because I have Manasi in my life. Even if she was not there, I wouldn't have anything to do with you.'

I pause before stating a difficult revelation. 'You are too

much like me, Vatsala. I see within you my anger, my ego, my ambitions, the same merciless determination. You love Bharatanatyam as much as I do. Two people mirroring each other are a disaster together. They are like two parallel lines, both of which might exist together but can't merge. Once you win me, you would lose interest. Nor would I have anything to build up with you. If we were to be together, our lives would be a mundane power struggle, each of us turning more and more self-indulgent.'

Not sure if I am speaking to Vatsala, or to myself. But I have to say this before the day ends.

'My life is compartmentalized with things that are close to my identity. I exist within some selfish ambitions. Manasi gathers up whatever I spread and presents them before me like a complete, unreserved whole. I move on very fast. She helps me to comprehend how well or how badly I have extended myself. She can see my insides even when I can't!'

I pause and look back at Vatsala.

'Today I have come to you asking for closure. As long as I reside in your heart, Vatsala, even without my consent, I won't be able to go back to my life in totality. Something, somewhere, would still be left with you in all those desires you have tried to bind me with. I want you to let go off me in your mind. Release my hold from anything that I may have touched inside you.'

There are tears in my eyes too. Vatsala stands like a corpse, waiting for me to finish and depart. I look her in the eye.

'It's not that I never needed you; it's not that I am rejecting you. You have given me one of the most splendid shows of my life. You have been instrumental in bringing to life one of my most distant, but closely desired ambitions. You are my first student in Manhattan. And,' I hesitate, 'You will never know how much you mean to me, and perhaps even Manasi. This, I can't explain. But it holds.'

Taking a few steps forward I touch her head with my palm.

'May you achieve much more than I have through Bharatanatyam. And congratulations. Kala Mandir, New York is ours.'

I turn towards the door, leaving Vatsala broken and shattered, alone with her tears.

Maybe she won't understand the depth of my blessings. But I am sure that someday, her art will give her the same peace and objectivity that I am blessed with today, putting into perspective everything that I may have distorted within her. Only to respect the spirit of an artiste, I felt it correct to address everything between us before the day fades away.

At the entrance of the hall where everyone waits, I stop abruptly.

Somewhere not too far away, I can feel Nobarun Bhattacharya smiling at me. An obligation that remained alive even after he was no more, has finally been fulfilled.

42

The Final Return

BRIAN HERRETT
Manhattan, 2016

The crowd talks among themselves scattered all across the hall, when a sudden loud cheer makes everyone turn. I look up. Shekhar has just entered the hall and he is mobbed immediately. Every soul today wants to touch Raj Shekhar Subramanian. Mechanically, I press the shutter of my camera.

Shekhar walks through the crowd, acknowledging the lavish praise directed at him. He smiles at everyone who wants to reach out to him. But he doesn't stop walking. Soon he stands right next to Manasi. For a split second, they both look lost in each other. The crowd is too caught up in the commotion to capture the little thing that passes between the husband and wife.

I have pressed the shutter again. This one is for my personal collection.

This evening Shekhar seems to have come back to Manasi like a free man. He stands beside her as her husband and not as an ambitious taskmaster chasing some inordinate goal. They look so complete together.

Joy is not only in winning over the impossible; there is also joy in giving. Perhaps Shekhar would never have experienced this, had Manasi not explained it to him in the language he understands best.

When Shekhar touches her, Manasi feels the change. She looks up at him, as he addresses the crowd and thanks them for their presence.

'What you have just seen is a performance orchestrated by my students. *Rasia* is purely the brainchild of Manasi, my first student, and others at Kala Mandir. My involvement was only of an executor; no more than that. It is an emotional moment for me to explain how my students have planned, conceptualized and brought this into being, now that they are well-trained, ready to take over the world, with or without me. What could have been a more auspicious start, as we are inviting students in an altogether new set-up, getting ready to re-start the same journey I started seventeen years ago.'

All his students rush towards him. The entire team of Kala Mandir is holding each other tight, with a tear in every eye. For one last time, I press the shutter.

This would be the story that no journalist has ever covered!

Acknowledgements

Journey of an author is personal. Stories we present are often a blend of truth and illusion. Yet, the one face in which I saw my protagonist, I'll start with thanking him first! You are a rare personality, Sir.

My literary agent Mita Kapoor, my editor Shambhu Sahu, and the entire team at Rupa Publications, much thanks for believing in *Rasia*. I owe my confidence to you.

I am thankful to my mother, Ratna Dasgupta, for building my interest in literature, art and Indian mythology at a very young age. I have never stopped reading since. Much later, a lot of my passion found answers in the books of Devdutt Pattanaik. God bless Devdutt ji; may he keep creating those hardbound wonders.

My parents, Sameera Sinha and Amarendra Kumar, thanks for all your support and love; I hope to inherit your strength and poise someday.

I wholeheartedly thank Somnath Kutty, son of the legendary Thankamani Kutty and Chitra Shankar, for feeding me with insights on something as deep as Bharatanatyam. Joy Sengupta and Soumyadipta Banerjee, my heartfelt gratitude for your constant encouragement in my writing career. Tanuja Chandra, big thanks for your kind reassurance when I was struggling to put my manuscript into perspective. Nazia Erum, thanks for sharing a very crucial information when I needed it the most. Thanks Priyanka Sinha Jha for all your support and for being a dear friend; it means a lot. Gaurav Gupta, Navjot Gulati, Runa Bhutda, Faridoon Shahryar, big thanks for the help you have unconditionally offered during the making of this book. Ranjan Pant, nothing that I have ever written has reached the third audience till I have taken you through my draft; I intend to keep it that way.

Dear readers, your mails and reviews keep me on my toes. Your verdicts are my rewards.

Just as the wanderer returns home after travelling across the world, my vagabond soul converges to the life I have designed with my author husband, Tuhin A. Sinha and my five-year-old son, Neev Tanish. Their contributions reinforce my faith in God, as planning–constructing–falling–failing–rebuilding–succeeding, all in the comfort of that constant support, makes my imperfections look graceful!

In fact, my stories have a meaning because my life has one.